AF413883

Black Gold
A Western Novel

Richard G. Hole

Far West 2

Oil was as fantastic a wealth as gold had been, and for this reason, it was not for nothing that it was known by the symbolic and somewhat ominous name of "black gold."

Oil was something simpler to discover and exploit than pure gold. It was enough to try your luck and open your mouth where the naphtha gushed out with overwhelming force, to possess the amazing mine that was to produce thousands and thousands of tons and with them, thousands and thousands of dollars, because it barely sprouted from the entrails of the earth the foul liquid, it was not necessary to keep digging day after day to extract the treasure. It was enough to organize the collection of the valuable liquid and exploit its continuous performance.

For this reason, as soon as the news of the first oil discovery spread, hundreds of men eager for quick riches, were amazed by the discovery and launched themselves to open holes with more or less fortune, because the subsoil was bursting with oil and he was wanting to expel it out of his gut.

Black Gold is a story belonging to the Far West collection, a collection of novels developed in the American Wild West.

BLACK GOLD

CHAPTER I

CRUSADE AGAINST BLACK GOLD

The entire huge gap that opened to southeastern Oklahoma with the rivers Muddy Boggy on the left and Kiamichi rivers on the right, was a lush green pasture for cattle. The combined effort of the various heroes of the territorial distribution of said new and last State of North America, had converted that reddish and rebellious land at first to pasture, after immense work, into an emporium of wealth for cattle and there were several ranches that were They had raised in the region increasing livestock in a State that, being relatively new when it proceeded to colonize it, required, given the increase in population that it had acquired, the help of livestock to attend to the maintenance of so many hundreds and hundreds of adventurers as they had settled in newborn Oklahoma.

At first, everything suggested that this suitable piece of American land would follow in the footsteps of neighboring Texas.

The land, once started up, was very suitable for livestock, and the settlers, as well as the ranchers, felt satisfied with the performance of their properties after the initial vicissitudes of their early days as pioneers of these lands, since nothing They had found a fit when they took possession of their plots of land, and they had had to lift everything by hand at the cost of enormous efforts and even heroic sacrifices.

And do not think that it had been an easy and risk-free task to convert the wild lands of the new state. To the fight with the hostile land, it was necessary to add the other more dramatic one with the unfortunate ones who arrived late to the cast and found no where to settle, and then with the various and dangerous bands of adventurers and livers, who under the cover of disorientation and the lack of both communications and authority, they tried to make victims of their plundering and robbery of the new owners. It took many fights, a lot of blood, and many victims to reduce this danger, establishing a principle of authority and establishing communication channels that linked with the border states.

But everything had been overcome with more or less difficulty and a time had come when the abnormal was neither more nor less abnormal than in other places on the continent.

But when these difficulties had been overcome, when those established there believed that the moment had come to enjoy the tranquility to which they had a well earned right and when it seemed that no other collective and explosive commotion was threatening them, capricious Nature set off a terrible powder keg, that although for many and for the nation it could even be a new emporium of wealth, for many of those settled there it was going to become a terrible threat and a new and bloody war that would last as long as one of the two contending sides fell defeated.

Just as California became a terrible hell the day that Sutter's carpenter discovered gold in his mill, so when one day someone digging the earth, raised the first oil well in those latitudes, the most complete The revolution threatened Oklahoma from its southern divide, with Texas, to that of the north, with Kansas. Oil was as fantastic a wealth as gold had been, and for this reason, it was not for nothing that it was known by the symbolic and somewhat ominous name of "black gold."

Oil was something simpler to discover and exploit than pure gold. It was enough to try your luck and open your mouth where the naphtha gushed out with overwhelming force, to possess the amazing mine that was to produce thousands and thousands of tons and with them, thousands and thousands of dollars, because it barely sprouted from the entrails of the earth the foul liquid, it was not necessary to keep digging day after day to extract the treasure. It was enough to organize the collection of the valuable liquid and exploit its continuous performance.

For this reason, as soon as the news of the first oil discovery spread, hundreds of men eager for quick riches, were amazed by the discovery and launched themselves to open holes with more or less fortune, although in many cases with fortune, because the subsoil it was bursting with oil and was eager to drive it out of its bowels.

Immediately, the smartest, the smartest, those who were always on the hunt for bargains, fell like legions of voracious termites on the places most conducive to exploitation and began the fight, the brawl, the more or less honest offer. or predatory for the exploitation of that wealth, that although being natural and spontaneous it flowed by itself, on the other hand it needed a rather complicated organization, to get the proper use of the product.

The product needed natural deposits to be collected, special containers to imprison it. Adequate means for transport and then refining factories to purify it and markets where to place it.

And this was too much for the poor settlers who, overnight, found themselves with a well or two, or several, leaking oil, which was lost without means of exploitation, since that start-up required not only capital, but all the complicated mechanics of its collection, transport, refinement and placement.

And as the agiotistas knew this, they tried to take advantage of this at the expense of the owners of the land and the nascent wells.

Exploitation companies were soon organized and contacted the owners. Some to acquire the land subject to a higher yield still hidden and others, when they encountered resistance for sale, reserving a part of the benefit to the legitimate owners of the wells.

As the number of people amazed by the oil began to form legion, and many wells were opened in a short time, it was a difficult task to go to all the places to take advantage of what was threatening to be lost, and the first to go to the claim saw and met each other. They wished, but soon, word spread, new exploiters came, money companies were founded to cover whatever was within their grasp and the start-up was normalized, fostering a new wealth that would give the State the greatest impetus, create millionaires almost overnight and would ignite the selfishness of getting rich to those who had not yet been lucky enough to discover a seam of black gold.

Adventurers as in the time of the Russ of California ventured with the peaks and the holes to dig the ground where they seemed best, without respecting dominion or property. New wells had to be discovered, and when the rightful owner of the virgin land opposed the invasion or tried to be him and not a strange hand who tried his luck, bloody fights and fights broke out, which began to form a census of the dead of one and the other part, quite terrifying.

As always, brute or collective force prevailed over weakness. Sometimes, when the invader was numerous, rough and organized, he would eliminate the unscrupulous owner of any species, and other times, when the invaded had the strength, he would shoot the intruder, or leave him nailed next to the wells he was trying to open. .

But, like gold, not all of Oklahoma was a naphtha deposit. There were lavish places, pockets where oil arose in any place where a hole was opened, but in others, the effort was negative, because the black gold did not exist there or it was so deep that it was not with a simple hole that could be used. force to flow.

According to studies carried out in this field, it is known that oil is in the opposite direction to water. This seeps downward and flees inland, and oil, on the other hand, has a tendency to rise and that is why, as soon as it finds the smallest opening of expansion, it rises with overwhelming force.

Oil appears to form in places called domes, that is, where the hollow earth has impermeable walls. In them, the pond, lagoon or small sea is formed, everything depends on the gap and there it remains until the first hole gives it expansion. Then, the dome is discovered, which can feed hundreds of wells, depending on the extent of accumulated liquid.

And since these domes are underground, no one can imagine where the oil is hiding. Sometimes, under the lush soil of the prairies, there are millions of tons hidden, and, instead, in broken or wavy terrain, not a single gallon was discovered.

For this reason, the discovery of black gold was more a matter of luck, although in some places, the bags were so extensive internally, that for many miles in length and width, it was enough to drill to see it emerge immediately.

These preliminary and empirical discoveries of oil in Oklahoma led people to believe that the search operation was straightforward, yet the general history of oil proves otherwise. As a sample button, we can cite the following. The Imperial Oil Company of Canada, one of the richest in exploitations of this type, spent twenty-five million dollars during twenty-five years, in opening one hundred and five holes of various depths, which reached up to almost four miles, and all with negative results, until one day, when drilling well number one hundred and six, she achieved one of the most reproductive finds in history, which compensated her for so many years of sterile work and so much expense buried in vain. If he had not had this last success, the loss for the company would have been terrible,

But these complications were to arise later, when once the deposits made to the surface of the ground were in operation, they were organized and our history sticks to the primitive time of the first wells in Oklahoma.

It is necessary to clarify that not all those settled in that area were infected with the black gold fever. On the contrary, there were staunch enemies of the search and exploitation of such wealth, because what for some was an unexpected source of wealth, for others it was something unsympathetic and for many a threat of ruin against which they were preparing to fight.

The outcrop of oil constituted a serious danger for those closest to such sources of wealth, in whose lands there was no gasoline or they had not wanted to search.

It was like a poisonous breath that dried and withered everything around. The land was impregnated with oil, the land became sterile, the grass turned gray until it died of juice, and the nearby livestock, which fed on the grass that grew next to the fields, ended up lacking pasture, when it was not available. he poisoned with what he ingested contaminated by oil.

For this reason, the ranchers who were now defending their business with the antlers, which had cost them so much effort and fatigue to carry out, felt invaded by a terrible unease with the oil invasion and not only did they not want to know anything about the new business, but also they had declared themselves staunch enemies of him. Those established in areas that the insatiable seekers had not yet seen, remained relatively calm, although in perpetual guard, for what could happen, but those who saw, alarmed, how the search advanced relentlessly towards their domains, threatening to saturate the earth, killing the grass and poisoning its bundles, they rose up in the face of danger and prepared to meet him.

The Wesley area had stayed away from the new fever, but the threat was not far away and all the settlers and ranchers in that part of the territory lived with their souls in a thread, pending the news that one and the other were transmitted regarding to oil activities at a distance.

Among the landowners and ranchers of that basin, the one who stood out most for the importance of his property and the large herd of cattle that he had come to gather, was Armor Fuchs, who when the invasion of Oklahoma left his position as foreman on a ranch of Texas to embark on the adventure, doing it with luck, since he had limited a large area of prairie with the help of two brothers who had followed him in the race only to help him conquer ground, although later, when Armor was consolidated, they abandoned that to continue in their businesses, which had nothing to do with livestock.

Armor shortly after took a small team from Texas, all belonging to the ranch where he had worked. He offered them better conditions than their old employer, and the laborers did not hesitate to accept the new job.

But they earned the increase well, because in particular the first two years, they had to fight with gangs of undesirables that lived off prey and assault, although later, as tempers calmed down, their mission was less exposed and calmer. .

Armor, who had left his wife and daughter in Texas, not wanting to expose them to the vicissitudes of that adventure, kept them away from him during these two restless years, but when he believed that the environment allowed them to be reintegrated into his property, he picked them up, taking them to the ranch he had built in the meantime.

Armor was lucky; the cattle were raised well, the offspring were prolific and in a short time he managed not only to gather several thousand cattle, but also to become the strongest and most prestigious rancher in that part of the state.

And since he had been born among cattle and raised among them, and cattle were for him his passion and his source of prosperity, he did not want to hear about oil, no matter how beneficial its exploitation was. In love with the pastures and meadows, he suffered greatly if he contemplated a parched or bare ground because of that damned oil, whose only smell seemed to suffocate him.

When the news of what was happening reached there and he advanced from the wells to the East, he was alarmed to the point of paroxysm. He could not tolerate neither that his lands were drilled, nor that the effect of the damned oil could affect his ugly pastures, endangering his cattle.

But ... he only owned his own and could not dispose of the land of others, or rule outside his property. Each one was very master of doing what he wanted with his own, although later, due to the natural effects of exploitation, someone could be damaged by rejection.

And to find out what his attitude should be and what forces he would count on if he were forced to face the danger, one day he summoned the various ranchers established in the vicinity and the settlers, who also counted in this case.

Armor gave them an exposition of the danger that oil was going to pose for them, against the problematic possibility that naphtha existed there. It made them see how calm they lived against the unease that was dragging behind them that fever of black gold. It could happen that in some piece of land there was oil and in the others not, in which case, the mere presence of a well that could benefit one without knowing who, could, instead, ruin others, since the earth would suffer the influx of that drying and deadly liquid, which could dry up the land, make crops sterile and destroy livestock.

On the other hand, if they joined in a tough crusade against any drilling attempt, they would gain more every day, because as ranches and fields invaded by wells disappeared, meat and cereals were scarce, due to the growth of oil and gas towns. Their products and their cattle would be sold better and at a better price, since the market of supply and demand was the one that set the price pattern and there was greater scarcity and need, more competition for acquisition and higher prices.

He was sworn in and promised not to lease, sell, or have a pickaxe driven into his land to find new sources of naphtha. If the others were willing to support him, he would put the strength of his team in the defense of that virgin territory, in favor of whoever it was, and they would defend him from any outrage or coercion, to force him to give up his lands.

If that was the case, everyone had to sign a document in which they joined and promised to prevent the invasion of the wildcatters that were roaming the places not yet exploited, in search of possible deposits to offer to the companies. All for one and one for all, and if they signed the document and someone was missing it, the mere fact of breaking what was signed, authorized the others to intervene in their property in the way that the common interests of the rest required. And if he, who was the one who owned more land than anyone else and had the best chance of owning oil there, committed himself to this, he gave a solid guarantee to the others, who had less chance of obtaining it. Instead, they would continue to take advantage of the shortage of wheat, feed and meat and increase the profits of their businesses,

The proposal was discussed, the pros and cons were studied and, finally, unanimously, it was agreed to form a solid front against the oil invasion and to sign the document indicated by Armor.

It was drawn up, among all, specifying well the bases of the agreement, to which each and every one committed themselves in their own good and in favor of the others, and once it was drawn up and signed, copies were also signed by all, so that each one owned one.

Armor was appointed president of that strange association, leaving him the initiative to confront any invasion attempt. Armor accepted, and for greater assurance, offered to augment his team with half a dozen more pawns.

If meat was rising in price, profits allowed for this increased expense and helped to reinforce the common defense, from which no one could be thrown out, if in any case the combined effort of all was required. Although at the moment the danger did not seem imminent, since the vanguards of perforators had not yet arrived in the vicinity, it was good to be prepared in case they appeared.

The agreement affected, in addition to Armor, three other ranchers, all of them further to the east, and therefore more in the rear of the advance, and six more or less prominent settlers. Among the ten, with the personnel at their command, if they did not turn their backs on them, they formed a force that could be a barrier against the expansion of that pestilential and devastating wave.

Armor seemed to be calmer after that pact. If they had left him alone, he could be suffocated by those around him if oil arose in that area, but now a very advanced dividing line had been marked, which would prevent the arrival of the seekers to the heart of that utter vain.

CHAPTER II

CHALLENGE

One morning in early spring, Virginia, Armor's daughter, had gone out for a ride across the prairie. The weather was magnificent, they had had annoying days of water or cutting wind and as the atmosphere settled down and the bad condition ceased, the glory of those spring mornings, so missed, invited to enjoy the serenity of the landscape and the pleasant atmosphere and caressing.

When he was walking a short distance from the ranch, scraping the fence of some fields that were beginning to appear very spiky, he discovered two horsemen advancing in the direction of the ranch. They both rode two beautiful chestnut horses, which they must have paid for at a good price.

The young woman stopped for a moment to observe the direction they were leading, and when she thought she was not mistaken about her intention to visit the ranch, she advanced to catch up with them. It was then that he recognized one of the riders.

It was Alvin Sekely, a man in his mid-thirties, tall and supple, good-looking, with a rather handsome face, and energetic, determined manners. A man who seemed to be showing that there were few things in the world that would oppose him when he was walking, when he took the straight path of a road. And indeed, he was an aggressive and unimpressible man, whose life was a pure accident, who had managed to overcome with determination.

From a simple farm laborer, he later became a cowboy. Although as a laborer he was nothing outstanding, he learned a lot about cattle and one day, when he found a person willing to expose a certain amount of money in the cattle business, he moved to Oklahoma and dedicated himself to running cattle through the towns of the State, where the possibility of obtaining fresh cattle that supplied him with meat had not yet arrived.

And he organized a route, which he later expanded to several. Thus, several times a year "once a month at least", he would acquire a couple of hundred bulls and, while driving, he would take them along the routes already laid out, and he would leave, one by one, or in more quantity, depending on the importance of each town, the horns it led, until they were all in place.

After this expedition, he started another one by different routes, and thus he was developing a business that gave him a regular profit.

Alvin had entered into an agreement with Armor to purchase some of these cattle, which he sold at retail, but provided him with a good deal.

Alvin used to show up at the ranch every two or three months at the most. He chose a hundred cattle, later sent the peons in his service to look for them, and disappeared to return when he needed new acquisitions.

It was from this that Virginia knew him, and for that reason he was hardly at a distance enough, she recognized him. On the other hand, she was sure that she had never seen the rider who accompanied Alvin, a man of about forty, well dressed, with an attractive and intelligent face, denouncing from the league that he was a man of excellent position and more accustomed to deal with people of viso, than with menial elements.

But what most caught Virginia's attention was Alvin's outfit, so different from what they always used to wear, that the remarkable change could not be overlooked. As a rule, Alvin dressed something more or less like a somewhat smug ranch foreman. It was a cowboy outfit in tune with the business he ran, although because it was more than a simple laborer, his clothes stood out for the best quality and the best care.

But this time, those vestiges of a man from the cattle ranch had disappeared. He wore an elegant suit, whose color harmonized with the horse he was riding. His shirt was no longer plaid flannel, but white, silk, with a plafond below the neck across the chest, and his boots, which were fitted with gleaming silver spurs, were shiny patent leather.

His flowered waistcoat, from pocket to pocket, wore a thick gold chain, with a horseshoe-shaped pendant and even on the ring finger of his left hand, he exhibited a gold ring, with a beautiful diamond, although its size was not excessive. .

Alvin, recognizing Virginia, took off his hat, now black, with a round top and not the usual one for cowboys and advanced the horse towards her, greeting her with a cheerful smile:

"What a great pleasure to meet you, Miss Virginia!

"Same here, Mr. Sekely. We hadn't seen him around here for at least four months. The other day he made my father notice.

"Indeed, I have been very busy during this time and it was not possible for me to come here, but just so you can see that I did not forget you, here I am.

"I celebrate it.

"Well, let me introduce you: This gentleman accompanying me is Mr. Kaplan, a great engineer and a man who knows horrors of his profession. Mr. Kaplan, this is Miss Virginia Fuchs: daughter of my friend Rancher Armor Fuchs, whom we came to visit.

Kapan offered his hand to the young woman, saying:

"I can assure you that I am not lying or saying any false flattery, if I affirm that I have had a real pleasure in meeting her.

"Thank you, sir, you are very gallant.

Alvin intervened enthusiastically.

"No gallantry; Mr. Kaplan has spoken a great truth. Tell me, Virginia, what do you do that every time I come here I find you prettier, something that seems impossible to overcome?

She, laughing, replied:

"It will be that with good weather, I wash my face more often.

"Very graceful exit, but you must wash it with the water of beauty at least.

"Sure you do, Mr. Sekely. I have a spring of my own and jealously guard it so that no one but me will use it. It has been a luck to find it.

"Do not say that. I think the opposite is the case and that it is the water that acquires the essence of beauty when you wash with it.

"Very pretty. Where did you learn so much gallantry and why did you keep it so hidden?

"The brush with people of high position, Virginia.

"Hmm ...! I can see that you have changed your usual attire for that elegant one. Or is it going to a wedding?

"What more would I like than to go to a wedding, but only one.

"What if it is not curiosity?

"To one where you were the bride and I was the lucky mortal to whom you were to say 'yes'.

"Bravo. That is the finishing touch to your courtship.

"I say how I feel.

"Well, stop kidding me. He has not answered the question, because I do not think that these clothes are the most suitable for walking among cattle.

"Oh, of course not! I'm not going to make it dirty by brushing against anyone's skin.

"So ... what's he coming for?

"I want to talk business with your father. Is he at the ranch?

"Well I do not know. I left there almost two hours ago and I have no idea where it may be.

"I wish to see you, Virginia. The matter is very important to both of us.

"Well, let's go to the ranch; If he is not there, I will send to the pastures to look for him.

"Thanks. You are always as kind as cute.

She did not want to respond to the compliment. He didn't like so much insistence on flattering her.

When they arrived at the ranch, the laborer guarding the yard informed them that the rancher had just come up to his office.

"I'm glad, because that way we won't waste time," said Alvin. Do you want to advertise us, Virginia?

She shrugged her shoulders. Two or three times, Alvin, despite his gallantry, had named her with a familiarity to which he had no right. Their relationships had always been superficial and he did not like it when no one took liberties to which he had not been entitled.

He climbed ahead of them and, stopping at the office door, opened it and looked inside. The rancher, seeing him, exclaimed:

"Hello, daughter, do you want something?

"Yes, Dad, to announce that Mr. Sekely is here with a friend and wants to see you.

"Very well, let it happen.

She turned and remarking the word, said:

"You can come in, Mr. Sekely.

Thank you Virginia.

"Miss Virginia... until now.

"Oh, excuse me! "He replied, a little cut off Alvin." I thought friendship ... Excuse me again.

And a little shocked by the touch of attention that the young woman had vibrated in his ears, he went to the office.

The rancher, seeing him dressed so elegantly, opened his eyes in amazement, and after the greeting, he commented:

"Devil, Alvin, I didn't know you from that elegant look. Business seems to be going well.

"IPhs! That business no longer interests me.

"That ... which one?

"The one with the cattle. I cannot complain about him because I have made a somewhat acceptable profit, but there are things that are outdated and I live with the dynamism of the times. Whoever does not do so, becomes outdated and loses their good opportunities.

"Aww! I didn't know ... what are you doing now, Alvin?

"I have become a wildcatter.

"How do you eat that with? I have never heard it.

"No wonder, stuck here and delivered only to your cattle, you seem to live very far from the reality of life and a man like you, who showed arrests and courage to come here, limit land and build and sustain this great property; He has more than enough conditions to become a millionaire with little effort.

"Now ... But I ... neither aspire to millions, nor do I like to make more effort than those of my initiative, which adjusts to my tastes and hobbies. I was born a rancher and I dedicate more energy and affection to cattle. Everything that cattle cannot give me, I do not want elsewhere.

"Well, I hope you convince yourself soon. For now, excuse me for introducing you. This is Mr. Kaplan, an engineer in the service of the Oklahoma Oil Company.

"So nice to meet you, just as Mr. Kaplan. The rest, if it smells like oil, I'm not interested.

"He is one of the most reputable geophysical engineers in the company.

"Even worse.

"I do not understand, but, well, we will clarify. And since you asked me what that wildcatter means, I am going to explain it to you. I suppose you are not so ignorant that you are not aware of the enormous revolution that is taking place in the State, with the discovery of oil.

"No, I am not ignorant.

"Well, it was an explosion like no one could dream of. It seemed as if the subsoil was willing to burst to throw out the seas of oil that no longer fit in its entrails and there is no place where a hole is opened, that does not end up spouting oil from it.

»Countless companies are being formed to channel production and collect that fortune in black gold, so that not a single gallon is lost. Among the various companies already in operation, the one I have mentioned is the strongest, the most organized and the one with the most operating elements. But, for the moment, she has felt overwhelmed by the enormous influx of wells and cannot dedicate herself to opening new ones, with the loss of time that can mean hitting them.

»But since it is not a matter of losing many and very good opportunities leaving them to others, they have leased many miles of land around the places where oil has sprouted and in others where their engineers have studied the terrain and believe that there are domes hidden containing large masses of naphtha and the question is to reveal it.

»This is the job of wildcatters. They call us that, because they consider us to discover oil by intuition.

"For example, I walk around a limited area and point out a place, saying:" There must be oil here, "and I modestly dig a hole on my own, but of course on company land and for it. I use a certain amount of time and a certain job, paying for it myself. If I fail, because there is no oil, or because because I am too deep I cannot reach it with such poor drilling means, the company gives me compensation to cover part of the expenses I made and then, I start again in other site. What about oil and did I get it right? Then, the company grants me a part of the profit reported by the well discovered by me, and if I don't want to and we reach an agreement, it gives me a total amount and I renounce the profit.

»As I am a determined man and I like to risk to win, as soon as this means of exploitation began, I gave up continuing to traffic in cattle and exposed my savings in digging wells in that way. I have been able to lose everything and I have been able to gain a lot.

»Until now, I cannot complain, because I have not lost, and although I have not become a millionaire, I have been lucky with several discoveries and I have collected an amount that would seem fantastic to another, but that no longer seduces me, because I aspire to earn much more.

»The proof is, you already see it. Now I dress well, I have bought a good horse, a beautiful ring, and I have several hired men who work for me in that regard. The thing has blown well and I am very satisfied.

"Very good" replied Armor, who was nauseated by everything that was talking about oil "and I suppose that his visit is due to realizing his good luck and telling me not to count on his livestock purchases for the future: I appreciate it Because now the orders, due to the increase in population, are greater and thus I will be able to serve others who urge me to provide them with more livestock.

Alvin smiled sympathetically and replied:

"No, I did not come to that. Actually, I think you should have cared very little about the beef business.

"For what reason if it is mine?

"Because there are others that are more productive and even more so when you own the amount of miles of land that you own.

"What does it mean? I do not understand you.

"Simply that I have come to propose a much more productive business than cattle.

"Which?

"The one with oil.

"It seems to me that you have been confused with me.

"Why? Is it a bad deal?

"I don't know, but for me, as if it were. Fortunately, so far the oil has not appeared here and it better not appear, because ... many things can happen.

"Come on, Mr. Fuchs, don't say such things. Do you know what it is like to be able to earn in one month what you would not earn in several years, despite what your ranch is worth?

"It is the same, I am not ambitious and, above all; even if it was. I want to earn money with what I do, with what I understand and like, not with those disgusting things.

"Money has no taste or smell.

"For those who think so.

Come on, Mr. Fuchs. Do not say that; I am sure that here, within the limits of your estate, you have many thousands of dollars.

"Has it hit you on the nose? I smile a bit of intuition for that.

"It is not intuition, but security and that is why I have come to see you. I hope you convince yourself that it is a good deal and we reach an agreement.

»It is true that the oil has not reached this far yet, but it will come, do not think so and precisely because these lands were still free of exploration, I, although it would be you from my intuition, I had the hunch that there could be oil around here undiscovered. This, for the first one to make it emerge, would be a great business and then, I spoke with some members of my company and asked them to lend me an engineer to do studies on these areas, and although the studies have not been done in depth, because for that a very extensive and expensive material is needed, the indications are that there is oil in these places.

And if there is, you, who have the greatest amount of land, are the most likely to be seen overnight with the emergence of a few wells, which would yield more than twenty ranches like this in ten years. We would all win, and the company I work for would rush to put all its economic power at the service of exploitation. Think about it, Mr. Fuchs, because the proposition is tempting.

"Even if that would be worth all the gold that is in the National Bank, I would not accept it. Only I know the affection I have for these pastures, what I have fought to see them flourish as they are and to see my fat and shiny cattle. I only know what this landscape is worth as a gift to the eyes and the value of its serenity. I would die the day I saw this grass that grew with my sweat withered and saw me wrapped in that nauseating smell that just thinking about it makes me sick. I earn enough with what I have, and I don't want more.

Alvin, annoyed, replied:

"And do you think that because you persist in that, you are going to avoid what is irremediable? You do not appreciate what I have come to propose to you, because what I have done with you I can do with any other colonist or rancher in the vicinity, and the oil would flow in the same way and the effects for you would be the same, but without benefit.

"You believe? Well, try to see if you are more fortunate with any neighbor than with me.

"Is it challenging me? Do you think that everyone will think like you when they see that they can make their fortune in a few weeks?

"I tell him to try and see if he can achieve what he cannot with me. I don't want to know about oil, I don't want anyone hanging around my land and applying their noses to him if he smells like that damn perfume, because the first one I see dedicated to that, I leave him nailed by gunshots.

Alvin stiffened. He had gone there sure of his success, had had an engineer accompany him so that he could begin his investigations, and had received the most resounding slap that could be applied to him.

Considering himself ridiculous for that attitude, he exclaimed incisively:

"It's okay. If it is a challenge, I will accept it and I will dedicate my efforts to locate oil in this area. I have offered you something that many would like, and you have answered me with an outburst. When you see oil being born at the edge of your pasture, then you may think otherwise.

"The day I see (if I see it and you do too), oil will emerge together with my parents and I am threatened with an attempt of ruin ..., it seems to me that someone will regret having remembered to come and look for it here. that he was able to search in less dangerous places. I will defend what is mine as the bravest would defend it, and take note of this, Alvin, because it interests you. If there is so much oil in Oklahoma, look for new sources elsewhere and do not come to threaten mine unnecessarily, because I will not tolerate it.

"Very well. I'm not going to look for it on your property, because I can't, but there is no law that prevents me from looking for it in other nearby places. There will be no other settler or rancher in this area who will be delighted with my proposal. You have made me consider a matter of self-love to look for you here, and as I am a man who never backs down when challenged to something, I will look for you and ... I will find you.

"Well, go ahead; I am curious to know who will be, of all this region, the one that accepts his proposal. I'm afraid you have too many illusions about that.

"Time will tell, Mr. Fuchs, and since everything we had to deal with is covered, I leave you.

"You do well, because it will be better for everyone.

"Who knows who it will be best for. Until we meet again, Mr. Fuchs ...

"Until we meet again... but not here, Alvin.

"The place is the same to me, if it is not here, it will be very close.

Stiffly, he left the office without saying goodbye, followed by Kaplan, the engineer, who hadn't been involved at all in the bitter discussion. His mission was to study the land where he was ordered, and the rest did not concern him. But he was not very happy with the interview. He had guessed that the rancher was a very rough man and he foresaw that if oil spilled in the vicinity and damaged his pastures, there would be war and it lasted.

CHAPTER III

DISTRESSING REPORTS

Virginia was in the yard feeding the ducks, which were swimming majestically on the stone basin, when Alvin and the engineer emerged on the porch. The young woman was curious to know what the smuggler had gone to, as she guessed that his visit was not related to cattle.

Therefore, when they advanced towards the fence, he asked:

"Are you leaving now, Mr. Sekely?

"Yes ..." Miss Virginia. Isn't that what you like to be called?

"Well yes, I think I have a right to it.

"Because it's me precisely?

"For being you and for being anyone. There is no motive or intimate relationship for anything else.

"Of course, especially when you are the daughter of a powerful rancher, and I am ... or was, a vulgar and poor cattle dealer.

"And that has to do?

"A lot of. Class pride goes to the head of many and many, forgetting that a large part came from lower layers. However, you may not know that I too have changed my fortune as your father changed when he came here, and that after a little while, I will earn so much money that I will be able to call the President himself.

"That is not a question of fortune, Mr. Sekely ..., it is a question of education and delicacy, and that ... is not bought with money.

"Maybe; But stupidity can be bought with money sometimes, and his father took all that was in Oklahoma. I came as a friend to propose a business that many would have envied and he answered me with a sovereign kick.

Are you sure that he did not answer you in tune with what you deserved? My father knows how to treat people according to what each one deserves.

“And you have been educated in the same school.

“I'm not his daughter for a reason.

"Well then, get ready to know about me as your father will know, so that you learn to know how to return favors and not launch stupid threats as if he were the only man on earth and the other vile worms that can be crushed with us. the foot. He does not want oil, which is black and yellow gold, although he doubts it, but he will have oil until the smell suffocates him.

"Is that what it is? If I knew about it, I would have saved you from having to take that kick that has hurt so much ..., or at least I would have given it to you, which would always have been softer, even if you think that mules are more dangerous than horses . No, my father does not want oil, and if it serves you some advice, take it: it is dangerous to try to put it in front of his nose in case sparks appear and someone gets burned with it.

“We are going to see that, 'Miss' Virginia.

“We are going to 'hear' that, Mr Sekely, and I have a feeling that some will be very disturbed by the noise.

She turned her back on her and started for the porch, while Alvin, with clenched teeth, followed her with his eyes and muttered:

“It seems to me that you are also going to enter the fight. I can't stand stupid girls of your caliber and who knows if you'll regret it more than me.

Virginia, tense, after her tense dialogue with Alvin, went up to her father's office. The rancher, possessed of limitless fury, walked like a caged lion through the narrow enclosure of the office.

The young woman, realizing her nervousness, exclaimed:

“Calm down, dad; a guy like that doesn't deserve to give much thought. Many things have gone to your head and you will soon realize that it is all just smoke.

“Do you ... do you know what he's come for?

"Yes; I've had an unpleasant conversation with him on the patio, and something he said to me and ... something he had to listen to. Do you think it is worth giving it importance?

"I don't know what to tell you, Virginia. I will only be able to find out when the solidity of the agreement that all the owners of this basin have signed is put to the test.

"Do you think anyone can miss their commitment?

"I do not know; I can only affirm that I will not.

"If the others have voluntarily pledged ...

"You have to know the human heart and its weaknesses, Virginia. When the danger is far away, we all think we are brave enough to overcome it, but when we have it above us, the value is usually very different. Until now, they have believed, like me, the issue of oil, not because it could arise in their properties, but because it could arise in those of others and not theirs, which would be what they consider the real damage. I think there are few who like me, want the land for what it is in itself and not for what it can hide under the pastures or ears. Perhaps many, if they had been assured that they were hiding oil under their feet, would not have signed the commitment; if they did, it was to prevent others from getting rich with it and they could, instead, be the victims of the neighbor's wealth.

"Yes, I think you are right, but if no one knows for sure that there is oil underneath them, they will not venture to betray their commitment and expose themselves to being the first victims of this damn affair.

"I dont know; Everything will depend on how they approach the battle and whether they look for someone's weak point. Anyway, don't play with me, it's dangerous. I was the first to be attacked in the name of all, and the first to have rejected it, although it would not have been difficult for me to allow them to open some holes to see what they found. If I have fulfilled the agreement, let the others imitate me, or by hell I swear that whoever does not comply with the agreement, I put the barrel of my revolver above his temple.

"Dad, for God's sake, don't get excited.

"I warn myself, Virginia. That guy Alvin is a poisonous snake and goes to your game without caring about others. It is very comfortable for him to try an experiment in my pastures ... they are vast ... somewhere he could be lucky enough to discover oil if it exists and then ... the move would be wonderful for him. Given the size of my ranch, a few wells would render him a great profit; he could even lease his land to others; This would be ideal for him, because although he would have exposed a handful of dollars to open a mouth, then he would only have to open his hand to start receiving money. The rest, work, upset, discomfort, even struggles, for the company, for me and for my neighbors. He, with saying to the company, there is the oil, come my money, I would have enough.

"What if he is wrong and there is not?

"He will spend a little of what luck has put in his pockets and to look for it elsewhere.

"That is exposed for him.

"Up to a point, for those who have little, they can lose little. On the other hand, arrogance blinds him and it has been enough to scratch him a little against the grain, so that he has curled up, launching his threats. I think that, out of pride, he will try what he would not try out of selfishness, and he has a lot.

"Let us trust that others keep their word and answer the same as you.

"That is what it takes, but just in case, I will have to maintain a tenacious vigilance and threaten again the weak in memory or poor in spirit. I have always feared the invasion of oil, but by its normal channels, by a chain of events that would bring it closer here gradually, or perhaps that it would not arrive, if between the closest places where it currently exists and this basin, they found a void that discouraged them. to continue east. What I never supposed was that the explosion fell on me by indirect firing, looking for me as a target precisely. Damn the time I met that guy!

"Let's wait calmly, Dad. To lose your nerves, there will be time if things take a bad turn.

"No, because what I must avoid is precisely that, that they can acquire a bad appearance. I have to get ahead of that guy and I will do it without wasting time.

And that same morning, the rancher, furious, prepared his horse and prepared to visit all the ranchers and settlers in the surroundings, who had promised to stand firm, not giving facilities to convert those fields and those green meadows into a black hell of dirty oil, bad smells, desolation and a nursery of rude and fighting men, given to the hard task of handling such a nauseating element.

When I walked through the green sweetness of the landscape under the caress of the sun, when I contemplated in the distance the moving note of the cattle browsing the grass gently, or the glory of the ears of wheat swaying in gentle waves, caressed by the morning breeze, He felt the rage of an erupting volcano igniting his blood, as he pondered what it would mean to see all that natural wealth destroyed, to turn it into a forest of rough wooden towers, vomiting jets of oil mixed with earth into the limpid atmosphere and turning everything into a dirty smelly and devastating quagmire.

He could not consent to it, he did not want to consent to it, and he would risk not only the estate, but his life in the endeavor. If instead of oil it had been real gold that the earth had enclosed, nothing would have mattered. Their pastures and their cattle would have suffered nothing, because around their property the earth would open until it was pierced from part to part, because the gold, neither stained nor spread, nor devastated and parched the bowels of the earth as a curse from God . It would have had the natural difficulties against the greed of the prospectors, but these struggles would have the same with the oil prospectors, in addition to the rest of the inconveniences.

The morning was lost making visits. Time and time again he had to explain the violent discussion with the former cattle dealer, his threats for not allowing him to spoil his lands and put the brand of discord in them, threats that he had picked up from man to man, to sustain them in the terrain that Alvin would like to consider.

And always his final sentences were the same:

"Nothing gives you the right to ensure that there is oil here. I was trying to prove it at my expense, to get ahead of the others, but I'm sure it's all an attempt to try my luck at random and nothing more. Now, just to get revenge for my refusal, I am sure that he will try to sow the weeds among all, assuring what he cannot assure, only to break our harmony. I hope that each and every one of us fulfill our commitment and that no one leads to serious consequences. We have weighed the pros and cons before committing ourselves, and the word of men must be kept above all else.

It was all he could do, and although no one dared to contradict him, he returned with the fear that Alvin had enough ingenuity to produce restlessness in the spirits causing some serious split.

The least of it was that it would make someone hesitate and force him to fail his commitment, allowing him to carry out a survey, the tragic thing would be if the survey was lucky and caused the catastrophe, which he was trying so hard to avoid.

From the reports he had acquired, oil was being exploited much more centrally. It was there where, for the moment, the focus of the fever was produced and where they fought and worked around the clock, to attend more or less efficiently to collect what was sprouting, as if the whole earth were hollow and the oil was struggling to come out at the first little hole that opened in it shallow.

According to some witnesses who had traveled some of the area, much of the sprouted was lost due to lack of adequate places to retain it until it could be collected. Huge jets gushed out, which then spilled out like pestilential streams, burning the land through which they ran, scorching fields and meadows, entering neighboring fields to ruin those affected and causing conflicts and fights, which threatened to reproduce in another sense. , what were the surroundings of San Francisco in the year 48.

These reports were received two days later, corrected and augmented by an eyewitness from that hell.

It was a nephew of Armor, son of a sister of his sister-in-law.

Joseff Fuchs, Armor's brother, was married to a Texan named Clara, who, in turn, had a widowed sister with a son named Gleen.

Armor's brothers tried to help the widow to get ahead until her son could help her and the one who contributed the most to this help was Armor, as he was the better off.

Later, when she heard about who the boy was and how smart and willing he was manifesting to make his way in life, she decided to help him get ahead and paid for his studies at McAlester, where he applied so hard, that to Forced marches, proving his ability and talent, he was finishing his law degree in half the time that anyone else would have used for his study.

Armor was flattered not only by Gleen's cleverness, but by his self-esteem for shortening distances and ending his career as soon as possible, being the least burdensome possible to those who helped him, and since he was also a fighter, he knew better than anyone else's appreciation. abilities of the boy and his brave spirit to break through in life.

Every summer Gleen, after a brief visit with her mother, would vacation at the Armor Ranch, where she was warmly received. Armor was proud of Gleen, because whatever the boy was in life, he considered it his doing, and also because he was an excellent and grateful young man.

And it was precisely Gleen who had just turned up at the ranch in anticipation of her vacation.

Perhaps due to too much study and work, he had been ill for a few weeks, accusing the effort, and the teachers had granted him a month's leave to recover. They knew that his studies were so advanced, that this break would not influence so that at the time of the exams, he passed his subjects.

Armor was surprised at his unexpected and untimely visit, but it was enough for him to observe that the boy had lost a lot of weight and had sunken eyes and sharp cheeks, to understand how much he needed rest and fresh and invigorating air.

"How are you around here so soon? "I ask.

"They have forced me to suspend my studies for a month, uncle" he replied. I had been very fatigued for a few weeks and had great headaches, and they recommended a month of rest, and I did not want to go to see my mother directly, so as not to alarm her if she saw me in this state. That is why I have come here.

"You have done well. After all, no one is pressing you to make that effort. You know that I help you with a lot of affection, because in addition to knowing that you are worth it, I know that you are not a lounger, but a diligent boy who wants to make you a man. It doesn't matter to me that it takes a year or so to finish your degree, but that you finish it normally.

"I have little left, man. I have passed two courses every year, and the next I will finish my degree. I want to do it, to settle in the capital to see if I am lucky and I take my mother by my side and I have just been a burden to you. It is a pity that you are not in a position to exercise it right now, because you have no idea of the lawsuits and fights that are taking place because of that stupid oil rush. I believe that if this continues, it will be necessary to recruit drowned in all the States of the Union, to bring them to Oklahoma.

"The pity is that they don't all burst and sink into their damn wells. I think that's hell.

"You don't really know it, uncle. I came from McAlester through the oilfield across the Muddy Boggy River and you have no idea what that is. Everything that was beautiful and attractive in the landscape has died turned into immense black marshes, which stink and make you dizzy. Fields that were about to bear fruit have fallen as the soil became impregnated with oil and poisoned the ears. Many pastures where he had cattle have become burned soil, and their owners have had to emigrate with the cattle to save them, I know of fierce fights between the injured and those who have found oil on their lands, precisely because of the damage caused to those who they have nothing to do with those wells.

The villages, once quiet, have become loose madhouses, adventurers from all over come to the smell of oil, some to work, others to live off it as it may. There is no place to be, life has become terribly expensive and everything is scarce; alcohol is on the rise and violence reigns everywhere.

»The exploiting companies try to get out of this oil babble, to take advantage of it, but reality overwhelms them. People are so foolish that they believe that everything is solved by opening a hole and making an endless stream of oil gush out, but then, when they have seen it being born, despair and troubles come. They have not foreseen the rest, they lack deposits where to collect it, it escapes uselessly everywhere, causing damage and losses at long distances, they feverishly search for a way to contain it by digging the earth again to produce lagoons that are filled before they open. As for the rest, I can tell you some things that I have witnessed that will give you an idea of what that hell is.

»In order to collect oil in some way, they look for vessels where they are, whatever kind they may be. I have seen a tavern robbed and the wine vats overturned to put oil in them, they enter the houses, seize buckets and other vessels for the same purpose, and each plunder is a fight or a fight, sometimes with spillage of blood.

»And the same happens with vehicles, whatever kind they may be, since they are essential to extract the oil and transport it to where it is refined, or to deliver it to whoever buys it raw.

»He who has the means, pays for the wagons at the price they ask him, the one who has no more than that, a jet of oil that once born again seeps into the earth for lack of means to collect it, struggles to seize them from shooting. The companies that begin to organize the collection, bring vehicles, which are sometimes robbed on the paths by those who do not have any.

»I have seen how some caravans of carts with containers come, escorted by men armed with rifles, who have to fight real battles with those who go out on the road trying to seize such precious material, and despite the influx of adventurers, there is not enough manpower to work properly in the wells.

»They offer them salaries they have never dreamed of, although the work is not paid for with anything, as it is the most painful and rude that I have ever seen. But money works miracles.

"They work like oxen and then, as soon as they get paid, they go to taverns to shake off the smell of alcoholic oil and get drunk and fight and they are like herds of buffalo roaming the streets of the villages. Something that has made my hair stand on end and has made me abandon that more than quickly so as not to feel completely crazy.

»I do not doubt that all this will be an immense wealth that will produce great benefits and will be very useful to the economy of the nation, but such gains and benefits can be forgiven for not supporting these damaging pictures and for the damage they cause to those who have nothing. to do with oil, nor do they want to know about it, which are quite a lot.

"It is sad and sad to contemplate what has been lost in that area stupidly. You, who are in love with the landscape, its pastures, orchards and flowers, your soul would fall to your feet if you suffered the torment of contemplating such paintings. It is something like leaving a paradise to suddenly find oneself in the bowels of a hell.

Armor, who had listened through clenched teeth, said deafly:

"You are right, Gleen; you have painted that as I have imagined it without seeing it, and just thinking that it can come here, I feel crazy and I want to take a rifle and start shooting with everything around me. I am glad that you are an eyewitness, because I am going to need your testimony so that you let some know that they will need it.

"Here? Fortunately, you are lucky that this is far away.

"That's what you don't know, Gleen. I have a few things to tell you about that matter, because I have a feeling that quite tragic events are coming and it is good to be prepared to face them.

CHAPTER IV

A PROPOSAL AND A FIGHT

Alvin went to Wesley with the engineer and asked for a room at the inn.

There reigned the most absolute tranquility and life did not offer worries or shocks.

When they were installed, they met in Alvin's room and the engineer asked:

"Now what are you going to do, Mr. Sekely? The company ordered me to accompany you because you had assured them that some verification work could be started on that rancher's pasture. After the reception you have given us, I do not think I hope to convince you to authorize it.

"I know not, but he has thrown a challenge in my face and I picked it up. I swear to him that if the subsoil of this space contains oil, I will drown him and his cattle with rivers of gasoline.

"Do you think it is worth it? No polls have been done here yet and it is not known if it will be found. You are in danger of burying here what you have earned elsewhere, just for the whim of fighting with that man, who seems too harsh to me. Just think that if, after all, you fail and cannot start probes or only open dry holes, you are going to be laughed at a lot.

"It is a lottery in which we both have the same chance of winning or losing. If he had treated me differently, perhaps he would have resigned, but he has been so superb that he even dared to say that I will not find here anyone who is willing to try my luck. It is believed that because he cares for his pastures and cattle and has money not to need more, others will despise the possibility of getting richer than him overnight. I want to show you that you are wrong and I will try next. Around here there are small settlers established very close to their lands. I will agree with someone, I will open some holes in their lands and if oil comes out ... what I am going to laugh when it slides through the furrows and gets into their pastures, scorching them and leaving their cattle turned into skeletons!

The engineer softly replied:

"If you are willing to do that, I cannot prevent it, but it seems to me that you have valued the character and aggressiveness of that man very badly. I guess you are very paid from your estate and if you make that move I am afraid there will be a waste of molten lead.

"I have my share on the revolver drum.

"Very good, then go ahead. What I do have to warn you is that either you provide me with a way to fulfill my mission, or I return to McAlester to place myself at the orders of the Company. My presence on other sites can be more helpful.

"Very well. Rest for today and tomorrow we will see what can be done.

Alvin was determined not to back down in his efforts to fight the rancher and defeat him as far as he could go in the attack and therefore, after studying the situation of the owners of the basin, he reported the names of the two settlers closest to the pastures of Armor.

With these reports, he conducted an inspection of both properties and decided on Steve Evanston's, whose land, located on a slight slope, seemed the most suitable, because if he reached an agreement with him and got oil, he was sure that the first thousands of liters that were lost until they could be bottled, would slide down the slope of the land until they entered the Armor shepherds, precisely on the middle part of the property.

This possibility made Alvin's aggressive black eyes glow like embers. He was stung by the haughtiness and threats of the rancher and even by the insulting tone his daughter had used with him. It would make them understand that he was not a meek enemy, who could be scratched without responding with a stomp.

Steve was working on his land when Alvin showed up. The settler looked him up and down in surprise and wondered who this smug fellow was.

"What did you want? "I ask.

"I suppose I have the pleasure of speaking with Mr. Evanston.

"Indeed, I am Evanston.

"So nice to meet you. Could you pay attention to me for a few minutes?

"Why not? You will say what you want.

"Well, you'll see; I am a member of the senior staff of the Oklahoma Oil Company, the strongest company that currently controls the largest oil production that springs from the soil of this State.

»My company is going to extend its business to various places that have not yet been exploited, and the closest to be exploited is precisely this area, because according to studies carried out in secret by our prestigious engineers, there is absolute certainty that in this basin there is a enormous and rich oil dome, whose ability to make many rich overnight, who today, to live fairly, have to work excessively all year long, earning much less. I have been commissioned with one of our engineers to study the terrain and propose the site or sites where you can proceed to open the first exploratory wells and as I am a man who has struggled a lot with poverty to make my way and earn money , I feel inclined to favor the most humble in this sense.

"For example. I could start by proposing to his neighbor, the rancher Mr. Fuchs, to start the work on his land; there is more possibility of exploration, enough wells could be drilled there and turned into a real gold mine based on the oil it contains, but it is not fair to favor the one who has the most, but on the contrary, to help the weakest, because wealth it must first distribute itself and help those who need it most.

"Around here, as I have been able to verify, there are some settlers whose properties should not yield much to them, including you and I have decided to contact one of you to give them this opportunity they deserve, due to their diligence and poor performance in their work.

»If it suits you, we can discuss the conditions to start the scan. I lease you a piece of your land and pay you more for it than you can use in a year. If by chance the attempt failed, you would have lost nothing. Once you have collected what you could get from the exploitation of the land and even more, the lease would be canceled and you would once again own your plot and continue planting it as you have done before.

»You tell me the amount you estimate that I should pay you and I pay it to you. Apart from this, if oil were discovered, the Company would be in charge of the exploitation, reserving twenty percent of the profits for it and if it did not want this participation, an agreement would be reached for the acquisition of its land. In any case, you would make a big profit and if you did not want to know anything about the oil, with what we gave you for your plot, you could acquire another ten times greater, in Texas or wherever you see fit.

»This for your greater guarantee, we can translate it into a contract for your peace of mind and so that you appreciate that we act in good faith, since it is a business that allows us all to win.

The settler, without making any comment, listened nervously, despite all that had been discussed with Armor and the rest of those seated there, the proposition was tempting. If oil was not found, since they would pay him in advance and in greater amount what he lost by not working the land, he would lose nothing, but on the contrary and if it was true that oil arose, then his fantasy began to fly, calculating the amount thousands of dollars it would produce.

But fearfully, he commented:

"Do you say that there is certainty that there is oil in this area?

"Of course. If not, why would we risk our work and our money digging useless wells? You understand that that would be stupid, there are areas where there is still much to be exploited.

"Yes, but the fact that there is oil here does not mean that it is precisely under my fields and that it is going to spring up precisely in the piece of land that you chop to look for it.

"When it is known that oil exists and above all, in quantity, the almost certain thing is that it will sprout where it is first provided with a mouth of expansion. For example, if behind that long bank, there was a water tank hidden, what would it do to open a hole in the part over there than in the part here, for the spring to emerge? The water would flow where the outlet was provided.

"Yeah right; in that you are right.

"Since you have understood, we can discuss the lease to begin immediately.

The settler, choking on speaking, because his selfishness had just been kindled well fed by Alvin's dazzling promises, said hoarsely:

"I understand that what you are proposing is very advantageous, but I find myself tied hand and foot to accept it.

"Why?

"Because I, as well as all the large and small owners of this basin, have signed a document in which we promise not to allow any exploration on our lands.

"Hey, what do you say?

"That's how it is. Mr. Fuchs brought us together, made us see the dangers posed by the oil issue and the damage that it could cause to some, although it benefited others, since not all of us were going to be lucky enough to find oil on our soil and we signed a document committing ourselves not to give up the lands for such tests, and even to mutually defend that no one came to turn the land into a muddy and destructive pool of what we have worked so hard to make flourish.

Alvin was biting his lip at the settler's explanations, and now he remembered why Fuchs had challenged him to try his luck with some other basin owner. He had them all firmly tied up and this was what he believed to be his strength.

And furious, he commented:

"And have you been so stupid or so naive that you have signed that pledge?

"You are right; the situation was painted in such gloomy colors that we thought we were choosing the lesser evil.

"By all the saints! How that vulture has abused his candor, Mr. Evanston. It has been the same as if a rich man knew that behind a rock there was a treasure and so that others did not take advantage of it, he told them: do not bite and look for him, because the stone may fall on them. What does it matter to him that you come out of your near poverty, if he has enough money to live beautifully? What he wants is for no one to threaten his own and live calmly with what he has, without further complications. That cannot be and you have to rectify.

"It's not possible; we are committed to our firm. If any of us fail to do so, the others have the right to intervene to prevent us from breaking the pact. For me it would be a commitment for others to jump on me, and invade my property, preventing me not only from trying my fortune, but even harming me in what this currently causes me.

"And do you think that everyone thinks like you?

"Not that I think that way. It is that I committed myself to that and I am obliged to fulfill it.

"What would happen if someone less scrupulous or less fearful than you saw things differently and renounced that pact? You can retract and in that case, you would have lost what someone else can gain.

"It is possible, but without guarantees, I cannot expose myself to the fact that there is no oil on my land and also to the reprisals of my colleagues for having failed to comply with the agreement. You say that you did not want to propose this to Mr Fuchs. Why?

"I already tell you; because they are the least deserving of help.

"And yet, before you came, you have been here to warn me that I would receive a visit from someone to make this proposal to me because he had rejected it. This being the case and giving him an example of formality, the rest of us are obliged to imitate him.

"What did you come to say that with? Fuchs is a liar and what happens is that he is angry with me for particular matters and fears the reprisals that I can take with him, I repeat that he is a liar and that I ...

Alvin didn't finish the sentence. Behind him, a young boy, tall, flexible, good-looking and properly dressed, had emerged, who with a cold accent asked:

"Who was talking about, gentlemen?

Alvin turned quickly and looked at the young man. He did not know him and did not like an intruder to interfere in his affairs.

"Is it something that interests you, friend?

"I don't know, it depends on who you are talking to.

"That is something that you do not care, because it is business between Mr. Evanston and myself.

"Very good, but there is talk of a third party and strong statements are made about him, do you want to repeat them?

Alvin angrily replied:

"And why not? I was saying that Mr. Fuchs hates me for particular reasons and this has led him to lie, saying that I had proposed to him before anyone else to look for oil on his land.

Gleen's fine but energetic hand quickly grasped the lapel of Alvin's well-cut jacket and the opposite fell brutally on his mouth, while the young man with a cutting accent, bellowed:

"Repeat that if you dare again, you pig liar.

Alvin, faced with the unexpected aggression, tried to shake off the pressure of that iron hand, while trying to return the blow to the thrown boy, but this one, who must have learned in the school where he was studying elements of boxing, evaded with a funny movement the direct that Alvin sent him and he replied with another to the right eye, raising in it a purple rosette with withering swelling of the hit part.

Alvin stirred and now reached to his side for the revolver, but Gleen wouldn't let him. Faster than he, he yanked on the holster with the gun, threw it away, and bellowed:

"The men who presume to be, show it by fighting with their natural weapons. Come on, defend yourself, I'm going to give you a beating that I'm going to take away the desire to return to throwing lies like the ones I've heard.

Alvin, blind with rage from the blows received and the ridicule he was running, tried to get rid of his rival, who was proving to be more dangerous than he seemed from his appearance and blindly launched himself on him, but agile Gleen, dominating the situation , serene and without nerves, he elegantly dodged all the crude attack attempts of his enemy and using his beautiful fencing as a puncher, he took advantage of all the opportunities that his opponent offered him, to apply blows and blows that demoralized the former trafficker and broke his strength until their energies are exhausted.

Spewing blood from his mouth and nose, accusing the purple marks of his opponent's hard knuckles, he snorted in anguish and emitted inarticulate grunts every time pain shook his flesh. He was taking a terrible beating, barely glancing at his opponent two or three times.

Until a punch received in the chest, he fell to the ground, where he gasped, as if the air was fatally missing from his lungs.

The settler, a little pale, attended the fight without intervening. I was impressed by Gleen's forcefulness,   which warned him that if he missed his commitments, he could be exposed to something similar.

Gleen, seeing the former trafficker almost destroyed, looked at him rolling in anguish on the ground and warned:

"This is a first notice you receive. If you don't know me, I'll tell you that I'm Mr. Fuchs's nephew and that I know everything. You have been to see my uncle to propose the same thing that he has come to propose here and you have been enraged when he refused and told him that no one would open their lands even if they locked up the value of the National Bank in oil.

"You threatened to try elsewhere and he told you to try and see if you could.

I wouldn't have gotten into anything if I hadn't heard him so blatantly disingenuous. You have come to these lands with deception, where they were already warned of your possible presence, but due to your lack of scruples, I had to intervene. I wonder what guarantees these settlers would have, if they allowed themselves to be seduced by their siren songs and accepted their proposals. The man who is so vile that he appeals to deception to achieve what he sets out to do, deceives even his shadow in all aspects of life.

»And now, it is better if he disappears from here if he does not want things to happen to greater. The entire basin has pledged not to allow wells to be dug on their properties and they will honor their word, or get what they deserve for their lack of seriousness. You are warned.

He took a few steps forward, took Alvin's revolver, and discharged it, throwing it at his feet. Then he added:

"The next time you bump into me, if you insist on staying here, do not intend to take this thing out again, because it is easy for your hand to stick to it and you will never be able to use it again. I truly advise you that I know how to handle a colt as well as I can handle my fists.

And turning around, he disappeared to return to the ranch, where they were ignorant of his tremendous intervention in the lawsuit.

CHAPTER V

ANXIETY OF FIGHT

Virginia was in the courtyard by the pylon when Gleen made her reappearance. The young woman looked at him for a moment and seemed to notice a certain disorder in the impeccable correction of her attire. Knowing how careful he was in that aspect of his presentation, he commented:

"What have you been doing that you come a little messy, Gleen?

He looked at his clothes and, realizing it, tried to correct the flaws.

"It could have been more, but luckily, it has not gone beyond a bit of unevenness in the clothes. I had a pleasant conversation with your friend Alvin, on the land of one of the settlers near your pastures and I could not avoid the small damages.

She immediately grasped the meaning of the boy's phrases and exclaimed, alarmed:

"Gleen, you won't tell me you stuck with him.

"Well, that is not the phrase correctly. I have not hit him, because I have not allowed him to hit me, but instead I have hit him.

"Why? Are we going to aggravate things more than they are?

"I don't know, nor do I care. What I do know is that whoever speaks ill of your father in front of me, or attributes falsehoods to him, that one, swallows the words and the teeth.

"How? Has that vulture dared to insult my father?

"Something of that. I was saying when I arrived that your father was a liar if he claimed that he had been here first to propose to my uncle the search for oil in his pastures and that he was trying to prevent others from earning money because he had too much money. I invited him to repeat those falsehoods and as he did, I crushed his mouth with a punch. The rest you can assume: he tried to turn against me, but he is so poor of resources fighting, as rich man handling his disgusting tongue and I have given him a beating that I have left him lying on the ground and half wasted, for a few days. I hope the lesson fits, but if it doesn't, the worse for him.

Virginia took Gleen's hands and said excitedly:

"Thank you Gleen, you have always been a good boy and very grateful to my father, who loves you like a son. I don't have to tell you anything else, because whoever loves my father loves me and whoever my father loves, me too. You have done well to come to his defense in that way, because if I had been a man and in your place, I would have done the same thing.

"I believe it, you are also brave and it is a pity that you were not born a man. Well, I mean, looking at things from your father's point of view. For me I am happier to have a pretty and friendly cousin like you, than a fighter and surly cousin. It is easier to understand you as a woman than as a man.

"Well, stop the gallantry now. What do you think is going to happen?

"What do I know, Virginia? It all depends on how that guy reacts and the people he can mobilize to look for complications for us. He alone could do little, especially if he cannot find people willing to allow him those tests that he dreams of so much.

"You are right. We will have to wait and see what he does after the beating you have administered to him. I would have liked to see how he was with how smug he was coming. He looked like a clean louse, he who has always dressed as a better or worse well-off pawn.

"You can figure it out, Virginia. At least, I can assure you that with the outfit he was wearing, it would be hard for him to show up at a meeting.

She laughed at the occurrence and Gleen joined in her laughter, being surprised in these manifestations of joy by Armor, who had just appeared at the ranch.

Pleased with the good humor of the couple, he went ahead asking:

"Is there anything left so that I can also take part in the party?

Virginia stepped forward, saying:

"I think there is still a lot left for you, dad. We were laughing at Alvin.

"From Alvin?

"Yes, above all, about how his brand new suit has been after the beating that Gleen has administered to him recently.

"How? What have you gotten on with Alvin?

"That I hit Alvin, man. I surprised him by insulting him and telling falsehoods about you and he did not dare to repeat them in front of me, because I closed his mouth with my fists.

At the rancher's urging, he told him about the incident and Armor commented:

"I thank you for that brave intervention, not only as a demonstration of what awaits him if he persists in making war on me, but also for what an example and threat it can mean for those who allow themselves to be overcome by temptation, if that vulture insists on Siren sings. Our success rests on each and every one of them complying with the agreement and it is good that they know that having been the first to reject the offer, they have the right to demand that others comply as I do. Anyway, I don't feel calm. Alvin is a bad creature and if he convinces himself that he alone cannot do anything I fear what he is capable of doing out of revenge. In situations as abnormal as these, there is no shortage of unscrupulous and adventurers who for a handful of dollars are capable of the greatest atrocities. It will be necessary to mount a severe surveillance around the entire basin, to avoid unforeseen shocks. They may not be able to search for oil on our lands, but they can produce attacks and cause severe damage to those who refuse to support their projects and if this happens, with what moral force can they be subjected and forced to suffer damages for supporting them? An attitude that, if I consider it beneficial for everyone, cannot everyone continue to believe that it is the best, especially if they are in danger of suffering severe losses?

"We'll watch, man. Precisely I have nothing to do during this month of vacation and it will serve as entertainment, while I ride a horse and breathe fresh air which is what I need.

Virginia protested:

"No, you don't wear an eleven-rod shirt, Gleen.

"Why not?

"Because if something were to happen to you, do you realize the responsibility it would be for us? You have a mother to watch over and you owe it to her.

"Good, but I also owe it to your father. What would have happened to my mother and me without the generous and disinterested help that he has given us and above all, to me, that if soon I will see my dreams of being something in life fulfilled, I will owe it to him alone? My father would not have done more for me and I would be ungrateful if he did not try to pay for that protection with the only thing I can afford.

"We have men at our service who can carry out that mission.

"I do not doubt it, but when it comes to exposing something, I am more obliged than they. They charge a salary for working and are not subject to more excesses, I do not do anything useful other than for myself and they pay me. We're not going to discuss that because you wouldn't convince me, Virginia.

The rancher, pleased by Gleen's words and by her firm determination and courage, replied:

"We'll study that, Gleen. We can all do something useful and it will depend on the circumstances.

Meanwhile, in the Evanston lands, he had tried to help Alvin, lifting him up and leading him to a stream, where he was able to wash his face, cleansing him of blood, but this was of little relief. He was sore, battered, full of bruises and wounds, and his clothes were half torn. Very poor presentation to be exhibited in public like that.

But he couldn't stay there. He needed a long rest in bed, for his head was spinning and he felt terrible anguish.

In a hoarse voice, he said to the settler:

"This is going to be the prologue of many things and very tragic, that are going to happen here. They have won the first trick, but the last one will be mine and everyone who is on Fuchs's side will have to regret it. For now, the victory is yours, but we will talk later. As for you, think about it while it's time. They have thrown me into the fight and there will be a fight until one of both parties is defeated. If when you are ready to return, you decide to break that commitment and second my plans, perhaps you will be the only one who wins, if you do not, then you will be one more to suffer the consequences.

As it was possible, he got on his horse and, at a slow pace, headed for the village. He had pulled the brim of his hat over his eyes to hide as well as possible his terribly swollen eye and some other injuries to his face.

He went directly to his room and got into bed, where he suffered the pains of hell plagued by the pains that tormented him.

At dusk the engineer who had been exploring the surroundings of the town arrived to get an idea of what that part of the State could give of itself as an oil basin. The anarchy that was reigning in other areas and that caused a lot of oil to be lost due to the lack of foresight of having adequate places in advance to at least dam it until its packaging, prompted him to study the possibilities of avoiding this loss there, pointing out the places where it could be improvised collection rafts, if the black gold could be found between the banks of both rivers.

Kaplan's surprise was great when he discovered Alvin in bed, with a swollen eye and countless injuries to his face.

“What has happened to you, Mr. Sekely? "I ask.

Shaking with rage and a little embarrassed by the confession, he had to give an account of his fight with Gleen although he tried to distort it by stating that he had been attacked by surprise when he was not expecting it.

The engineer commented:

“I already warned you that this man seemed too harsh to me and also he is not stupid. If you have committed all the owners of the space not to allow the explorations and also have men to intimidate them and force them to comply with the agreement, little or nothing can be done here. Why don't we go away or try that in more favorable places?

“Because I have already made a question of self-esteem to fight with that guy until he is down. If he has power, I will show him that I can also mobilize another similar one and we will see who wins the battle. As the situation has been, my vanity is willing to sacrifice everything to win the fight and I would give all the benefit that oil could bring me to discover it here and ruin that guy. I have a stake in several recently discovered wells and I am going to get in touch with the Company so that they can buy that stake from me and give me the amount. I will use it all to act in this area, until I use up the last dollar or go down fighting hard.

“Very well, that is something that since it only depends on you, I cannot intervene in it. My mission here for the moment is over and I'm going to McAlester tomorrow. If it were necessary to return again, you will give me the order, because for now I do not think you can solve anything, and you will even have to stay in bed for a few days until you are ready to come out again. Anyway, I don't know what you can do if everyone refuses to let you dig wells.

“I will open them where those people's property ends or send a legion of adventurers to shoot them open. The procedure matters little to me, as long as I achieve what I set out to do. In any case, I have conceived a half project that if it works, perhaps it will be a shadow blow against Fuchs.

"Can it be known if it is not a secret?

"For you it is not, since you are as interested as I am that the more oil the better. My idea is one: if because of the commitment no one dares to miss it, on the other hand there may be someone that if they buy their property at a good price, no one can prevent them from selling it. As long as I only find one willing to sell it to me, I'll have enough for the test.

"Yes, it is half a solution, because if oil is not found, what do you want that land for?

"I would sell it again, even if I lost money on it. There would be someone who, having the assurance that this would not be threatened, would acquire it to continue cultivating it. You know that not everyone has a penchant for oil.

"Agree. You do what you want with your money, but think about it. He is going to get into a fight in which he could lose what he has won at the cost of exposure and work and can also lose time and with it, opportunities to continue exploiting the luck that has accompanied him until now as a wildcatter.

"If it is true that luck is with me, the same can accompany me here. You are not unaware that this is a gamble in which we risk everything blindly. That being the case, what difference does it make in one place than in another? But bear in mind, that if I reached you here where no one has come to explore yet, as soon as the first well brought out a little oil, my luck would be completely cast because I would get ahead of everyone and lease all the land to the Company. . You are not ignorant of what happened in East Texas. There were many years in which geologists were affirming that there was oil there but nobody could find it. Several companies joined, spent millions uselessly and finally, not so long ago, a humble wildcatter who risked his money drilling wells, two of them dry, when he was spending his last dollar to open the third, . Why should I not have the luck of that predecessor of mine, who through audacity and courage has become in days much more than a millionaire?

"True, but what about those who have used what they had and lost it without making a profit?

"We go back to luck. If I have it as it has been shown up to now, I do not want to upset it. That she follow me where I take her, which is her obligation

"Perfectly. After what has been said, I have nothing left to say, except that it is one thing to fight alone against the unknown of what the earth keeps in its entrails and another to fight against the armed will of many men, willing to prevent that from being attempted. It is a double chance to run and perhaps it is demanding a lot from that luck that has accompanied him until now.

"We'll see. Nothing has been written about cowards and I am not, although from the traces it seems that I let myself be overwhelmed by anyone. These blows I will return in spades and for some they will be more painful.

"So if you want something for McAlester, let me know.

"Yes; talk to Mr. Qualen and ask him to study the amount they can give me for my participation in the wells discovered by me. Tell him to price it as high as he can, because it is money that I am going to use in the same and that if I am wealthy, what he discovers will be offered to the Company and not to any other. Keep in mind that if oil comes out here where competition hasn't come, business can be great for Oklahoma Oil Company.

"Don't worry, I'll tell you so.

"I don't think I need to tell you about the incidents that happened. This is a particular matter of mine outside the business, which cannot have an impact on the company. And in a week, I hope to return there to finalize our deal and return to this place to start the battle again.

The next day, the engineer left Wesley to return to the Company's offices to give an account of his mission and to present what Alvin had commissioned him to do.

The engineer was less optimistic than the former dealer and had a feeling that Alvin, out of pride misunderstood from the beginning, was going to get into a hornet's nest that could be his moral and material ruin.

But despite this, I admired her mettle and determination. Oil, like gold, was proven to be a business of daring and strength, where the toughest and most risky had a great advantage to win. In this sense, the wildcatter had the nerve and the grain to deal with a situation as thorny as that.

CHAPTER VI

LOVE FROM DIFFERENT PLANES

Almost two weeks passed without Alvin showing signs of life again, and nothing noteworthy happened.

But since Fuchs did not trust Alvin, he had mounted a special guard, who would scour the prairie watching for any suspicious movements that might occur.

Meanwhile, Gleen, who only needed to forget the books for a while and breathe fresh air by exercising outdoors, was recovering from his small weakness and becoming stronger and more spirited.

To distract the boredom, he often rode horseback with Virginia. Gleen was very attracted to her, although she was careful not to go outside the normal limits imposed on her by her special situation with respect to her uncle and protector.

He owed him everything, he lacked everything, and he could only hope to one day be a prestigious lawyer and earn money, but this was still a long way off.

Virginia, too, had a fondness for the boy. He had had many occasions to touch his various sensitive fibers and he tasted good, studious, with noble eagerness to make his way in life and this coupled with the fact that he was pleasant in dealing, witty in conversation and, furthermore, a good kind of man. , greatly influenced this attraction.

One of the mornings they were strolling through the lonely meadow, Gleen commented:

"This seems to have calmed down, but I don't trust much. I suspect that it is all due to the fact that I left that toad to remain hidden in a hole for many days and that it is only waiting to be in a position to bring its stinger out into the sun. I would feel that all this exploded when I was forced to return to my studies.

"Why?

"Because I would like to take part in the ruckus. This is something that does not come easily to a poor law student.

"You fight with the Code in hand and I don't know if you are more fearsome with that weapon than with a .45 colt.

"There is no exaggeration, Virginia. We defend the right of those who are attacked not with firearms or sharp weapons, but with bad tricks that can only be counteracted with the application and interpretation of the Law.

"Don't tell me that everything you defend is always fair. Is there a person superior to a lawyer, capable of wanting to show that white is black?

"Well, maybe it's not all white, but it's not completely black either. At most, we can be criticized for highlighting more the part of color that we are interested in defending.

"I don't like lawyers, Gleen.

"We are not all ugly" he said with intention ", some are even handsome and elegant.

"Do not lower yourself, because I will not be the one who officiates in this case as a lawyer, highlighting the part of color that best suits you.

"You are wrong and I am sorry, because what better lawyer could I find for my poor lawsuits?

"I was not referring to the type, but to the profession.

"There has to be everything in the world, Virginia.

"Why and for what? There are tigers and lions and poisonous snakes, do you want to tell me how useful they are to humanity?

"In a Zoo, they are always an exotic and distracted sight to the eyes.

"In that case, let them also put the lawyers in cages so that we can see them as vermin reduced to impotence.

"You are terrible, Virginia.

"I say what I think. I do not know why my father when he decided to help you, did not bring you to the ranch and imposed on you in his tasks as was logical. You would have learned to understand this, to defend it and to fight for it with its courage.

"Do I intend to do anything other than fight for it?

"Not; you would fight for my father and for me, which is not the same.

"For you and your farm, from which I have extracted what I did not deserve, in order to continue my studies. Don't say things that hurt me.

"You do not understand me. I meant that here you would have been useful to yourself and useful to my father.

"If he had asked me, I would have loved it, but your father knows enough to defend your property and he wouldn't. If he had brought me here, I would have learned everything about cattle, but logically, what would I have gained in my position, no matter how high it was? A decent salary nothing more, because everything that would have given me more, it would be gracious for being his nephew, but not for my position. On the other hand, as a lawyer, you earn a lot of money if you show that you know your profession and are ready to defend difficult causes. Large companies, which always tend to have major conflicts, are looking with interest for someone who stands out in this regard and I aspire to one day be a lawyer for one of the most prestigious companies. When that comes, you'll see if I'll make a fortune in no time.

"I will be very happy for you. Since you have embarked on that path, my wish is that you get to have a palace in Oklahoma.

"When I have it, I will invite you to come live in it.

"Do you think that I serve to look good in good society?

"You serve to outshine the prettiest and most distinguished women who can appear anywhere.

"Isn't that the eyes you look at me with?

"The eyes with which I look at you, would say much more, so much so that there would be no words to translate it.

"Stop the report, Mr. Lawyer, it is unhinged.

"No, because I am defending a lawsuit that may affect me.

"Yes? In what sense?

He, after a moment's hesitation, replied:

"Listen, Virginia. If I finished my degree next year, if I quickly proved that I am worth more than many and managed to be hired by a great Company that gave me a fabulous salary and an enviable social status, would you have a problem in being the wife of that prestigious lawyer?

She also hesitated before answering and finally said:

"I would not accept it.

"Why? He asked painfully. For me or for my career?

"For your career.

"What can you oppose to her in the conditions that I have explained to you?

"I only have to oppose one thing. A magnificent ranch to which I will be heir and in it, a home that I love with excess.

"But, do you realize that you are a young, beautiful, attractive and elegant girl and that here you consume yourself in a very large and very open cage, but a cage at last, without distractions, without society, without those joys that offers the world and that for a woman like you, they have to be the biggest attraction?

"It is possible, but this also has its charms. I like to ride a horse, travel the landscape, breathe the pure air of the prairie, or the pastures and feel like the owner of the cage that you mention, without anyone getting into it if I don't want to and without the conventions and tyrannies of the life of society.

"If I agreed to marry you under these conditions, have you thought about the kind of life I would be forced to lead? She would be the wife of the great lawyer, who would only have time if it came to him, for his lawsuits. He would spend the day from one place to another, looking for papers, data, evidence, taking statements, defending lawsuits and the nights, he would have to steal many hours of sleep to prepare his reports, his defenses, remember such and such articles of the Code, Interpret them, twist them, tame them in his own way and he would end up going to bed tired, exhausted late at night, to get up early and start the same thing again.

»If we had children, you would see them in passing, a kiss and remove them from here, they disturb me, they do not let me work, I have to prepare this report for tomorrow. It would be better to send them to a boarding school, where they become men for tomorrow, men as machines as their father to earn money and not be able to enjoy it, to their liking and even to not be able to dedicate more than small and fleeting moments to their wife and this sometimes, sacrificing a rush job or something similar.

No, Gleen. As a man I appreciate you very much, I think you would be an ideal husband, but as a lawyer I hate you and I don't want to know anything about those ambitious plans that would turn you into an automaton and me into a martyr.

»I want a man of absolute freedom, here in these pastures, on horseback, running them at a gallop, taking care of the work of his laborers, directing it, whatever you want, but free of movement, because all that would not prevent me from being at your fingertips. side constantly, because for that there are more horses to ride alongside you.

And then, when the sun went down, when when the afternoon died, the cattle would rest and need neither your vigilance nor your effort, then the sedative peace of the ranch, dinner at fixed hours, without frights or haste, without reports urgent that everything be run over and if there were children, more than enough time to care for them, to caress them, to play with them and put them to bed gently rocking them until they fell asleep.

»Do you realize what that means for a woman who does not want money because she has it and who, on the other hand, would want unrestricted love, have the loved man by her side at any time and know that she is happy, agile, strong, without worries, without consuming your eyes under the light of the lamp until dawn interpreting articles of the Code for the benefit of others?

No, Gleen, no. I interpret love and marriage this way and I won't admit it otherwise. I warn you so that you do not get very logical illusions in the change you have undertaken, but very different from the one I am leading.

Gleen, who had become tense when he heard her, exclaimed:

"Virginia, do you realize what it would be like to tell your father that I was giving up my career after the sacrifice and expense he has made to get me to finish it? If he even had the money he spent on me to repay him, there would be no harm, but this way ...

"I am not asking you to throw your future out the window, Gleen; You have thus made a point-blank proposition to me and I have hastened to expose you my views on the matter. As there is nothing to go wrong so you can have an idea of what would happen if you take that idea seriously.

"You think he wasn't serious?

"It's one thing for you to mean it and another for you to be serious. You have a future ahead of you almost at your fingertips and it is not your career that you have to sacrifice a woman, but on the contrary, although not even that, because I am sure that there will be many who think differently to me and for them that is the height of happiness. When you have made your dream come true, you will not lack the woman who harmonizes with your office, with your embroidered sneakers and with your evening dress when the second centenary of the proclamation of our independence is celebrated.

"Don't be sarcastic, Virginia.

"Is not that; is that I want to reduce drama to this situation a little silly.

"You will say a little cruel. I have always harbored the idea of being able to capture your love, if you wanted it to be so and your father accepted it. Understand that I would have no right to simply pretend to you, especially what your father has done for me. It would be as much as supposing that I intended to win the saint and the alms.

"I understand your scruples and your views; I hope you understand mine in turn.

"It's so hard for me to understand them ...

"Of course, because as a future good lawyer, you want to resolve the lawsuit in your favor, without taking into account the reasons of the other party.

"No, Virginia, God knows that it is not because of that, but because I love you and for me, it would be a spiritual failure to lose the possibility of that love, not because there is something in my person as a man that repudiates me, but because of those prejudices social claims you claim.

"Life prejudices, Gleen. I have painted you a situation as I imagine it and if you were a woman, you would think as I think.

"It is always exaggerated.

"Sometimes in favor and sometimes against. Perhaps reality would show that I had fallen short in drawing that panorama.

"I would try not to make it as bleak as you imagine it to be.

"Perhaps at the cost of sacrifices on your part and of not fulfilling your work with the necessary intensity. You would suffer a lot before such an alternative and I am not so selfish that to satisfy my tastes, I try to bend anyone to sacrifice their needs.

"I see that you are irreducible.

"Who knows if you can change.

"Who knows if you can change yourself.

"I have given you a reason that chains me.

"Well, drag that chain or break it if you can. I think we should drop the subject, Gleen.

"If it's your taste ...

"It is not taste, it is a necessity and a good for both of us. Why torment yourself by turning over unsolvable problems? You have a beautiful future ahead of you and you will not lack worthy women. Maybe the daughter of an oil or banking magnate falls in love with you and one day we see you as a senator or something else.

"Don't mock. I have no ambitions to appear.

"You are obliged to have them in that sphere. As you will not have them, it would be put in those pastures, taking care of a bunch. I can find a man if not the same, something similar, that in exchange for not being able to give me some things, he gives me others that are closer to what I want.

"It is that I do not make myself think that one day you could be in the arms of another man.

And what about you from another woman?

"I only aspire to one of yours.

"They are also in chains, Gleen. They could not welcome you as you wish.

"Oh, you are cruel!

"I am sincere, why should I cheat on you?

The lurid dialogue was suddenly cut off. They had reached the ranch and Armor, who was returning from the pastures, was cutting off their path.

The rancher greeted them with pleasure:

"Hi guys, going for a walk?

"Yes Dad. We have done our turn to watch; Quiet on all fronts, Mr. Fuchs.

"Lower your hand, Sergeant" said Armor, observing the girl's military gesture, bringing her pretty hand to her temple in a comical regulation salute.

"At your command, my captain.

"We have not observed anything abnormal either. I can't explain Alvin's silence.

"Maybe one day he will cry out to get even for all the time he has been inactive.

"It's possible. In any case, I have walked around the basin a few times and have spoken with the settlers and ranchers, but no one has received visits of that nature again.

"Well" Gleen replied, "I think it's better to wait and see where she breathes. If something is to happen, I would be glad if it exploded soon, because I would be sorry to leave and that my poor help would be needed.

"It better be that way, Gleen. It could touch you something you don't need and spoil your future. I don't want responsibilities to your mother and I even think that now that you've recovered a bit, you should go see her.

"I won't, because it would scare you. He does not know that I am enjoying this vacation and he believes me studying. When the summer vacation comes, which will not be long, then I will go see her and there will be no need to stir her up. My mother would not believe that I am already well and would live tormented by the suspicion that I have some internal evil. I know her very well and I know what she would think.

"In this I do not force you to do what you do not consider appropriate.

And the three of them went inside the ranch, without Armor being able to suspect the agitation that engulfed the two young men.

CHAPTER VII

A SUCCESSFUL TRICK

Suddenly the first stone-laden cloud loomed over the calm. One of the settlers, quite close to Fuchs's ranch, came to Fuchs to talk to him.

The rancher guessed that something serious was beginning to float in the atmosphere and staring at him, he asked:

"What did you want, Mr. Long?

"Just tell you something that I find very interesting. I, like everyone else, have promised not to allow any well to be dug on my property to search for oil and I understand that when a man commits himself to one thing, he must fulfill it.

"I am glad that you think so, Mr. Long.

"I think like that, but between thought and reality, there is a gulf.

"What do you mean?

"You know that you are putting pressure on each other, looking for the weak point from which to arrive at that possibility of looking for oil here. It is necessary to suppose that the indications that they have on him are very safe to demonstrate that interest in making it sprout here precisely.

"That would have to be talked about.

"Maybe, but there are more immediate realities. A proposition and a threat have been made to me. The proposal is to buy my property at a price three times higher than the natural one. If I do not accept, I am threatened with a series of sabotage and intense reprisals, until they achieve what they have proposed.

»And you must understand that someone who is relatively poor, since my property is modest, cannot be exposed to one day burning my crops or poisoning my lands so that they do not produce and who knows if they might even stalk me to shoot me twice. his back and suppress me as an obstacle to his ambitions.

"As far as we know, the oil find story is a second edition of the gold find. Passions are unleashed, selfishness explodes and all means are good to achieve the objectives.

And this is my dilemma. I am not capable of breaking my commitment, but I am not willing to be ruined or taken out of the way. For this reason, the most practical way of fulfilling my commitment and avoiding harm is to accept the purchase offer that they make me and go from here to another place,

»I have promised not to allow wells to be dug in my fields, but I have not promised not to sell my property if they pay me well and I am going to sell it.

»But before that I have believed it a duty to inform you of the situation so that you are prepared. You have waged a struggle with elements that perhaps you have not calibrated well and perhaps you have the strength to accept that struggle. I do not have them and I withdraw before being a victim of this struggle.

Fuchs, who had listened through clenched teeth, said harshly:

"Long, why are you such a coward?

"It will be because I was born that way. I am not a coward, but I am not a hound either. A damage always comes out of every fight and can be faced when that possible damage is less than the compensation, but when it is not, it is foolish to fight, expose and lose. If they give me three times the value of my lands, I avoid struggles, dangers and losses. I can settle in a quieter place and live better. What do they find oil? Well for them. What fail? Well, hold on, since they wanted it that way. I will have saved what is mine and no one will be able to accuse me of being a traitor or a fool. And this is what I have come to tell you. They have arranged to return in two days with the money and the deed to take possession of my land. As sold they are no longer mine, I do not break the pact, if someone is missing,

Fuchs was roaring. He understood the settler's reasons and did not know how to step out to fill that terrible gap.

Because he could, by making a sacrifice, buy his property from the colonist at the price that Alvin paid him, for he was sure that it was Alvin with the money from the exploiting company behind him who was making that offer, but what would he get by stopping this blow and use the money in that land that was of no use to him, if there were nine other owners in the basin and the offer could be transferred to another and to another, until they were all resorted to? He would have to buy all the land for miles around at three times the price, and he didn't have the money for that much.

Therefore, he tried to convince the settler not to accept the offer, promising to protect him and his crops to avoid any retaliation.

But the colonist was not convinced. The effectiveness of that defense was very problematic, but even considering it as safe, there were other dangers against which they did not warn him.

One was that if they found oil somewhere else and it turned the basin into an immense lagoon, their land would dry up and if later on their plot did not come up oil, they would have lost everything. The other danger was that at that moment he could have three times the value of his lands without fighting and then he could have nothing.

Therefore, I saw no other solution than one. The acquisition of your property by whoever pays the best.

Fuchs, overcome by a dull rage, replied:

"Okay, Mr. Long. Since we still have forty-eight hours to study the matter and decide, we'll talk.

"Very well. As you will appreciate, first I have resisted the offer to rent a part to try the test, losing that money and who knows if even the finding of oil in it, which would have been worth more money. I wanted to be faithful to everyone and to myself, but when things take on that turn and threat and great loss enter, it is very human to guard against all that.

"Okay, Long, I take charge of your points of view and I cannot censure you, because if I have a criterion I cannot impose it by force on others. I thank you at least that you have advised me of your decision so that I can study the means of preventing it. Perhaps you have not considered what this sale can mean for the economy and the common welfare, but it is logical that everyone sees things according to their convenience. I only know how to tell him that all this was born out of a personal struggle between me and that trafficker who represents the oil tankers, and that oil has nothing to do with it, because in reality, neither he nor anyone else knows if it exists here. He wants to try his luck as he has done in other places and wants to ruin me if he can, using oil as a weapon. What will be the end of the struggle I do not know, but I can assure you,

"I take care of your attitude, Mr. Fuchs, maybe if I had a ranch like yours, I would think the same.

The settler prepared to leave. Fuchs warned:

"I hope to see you before everything is finished.

"I will be glad that you find a workable formula that satisfies your views.

A little later, the rancher told Virginia and her nephew the disturbing news that Long had just communicated. The three looked at each other uneasily.

"What do you think can be done, Dad? Virginia asked. We had not counted on that.

"Not really. However, I always feared someone's defection, although in this case that man uses a right that no one can deny him. If he knew that only he and no one else was capable of being seduced by such offers, he would lose that money by buying his land, but I fear that as soon as this happens, the offer will be made to another and that other accepts, with which a chain would be formed. that I am unable to bear.

"I understand. What are you going to do?

"I am going to gather the others and give them an account of what happens. I'm afraid this is an explosive bomb and that many, if not all, are inclined to imitate Long, trying to sell their properties as the lesser evil. If this happened ... do you realize my situation? I would see myself in a terrible circle, with no other possible salvation than one: that there was no oil in this area, but if it did exist, it would be my ruin and the absolute triumph of that pig.

Gleen, who had remained tense while his uncle realized this terrible threat, intervened to say:

"Uncle, I think that if the remedy is going to be worse than the disease, you should not tell anyone or give an account of what is happening. It is preferable that this thread of the fabric we try to rebuild it ourselves, without exposing ourselves to the other loose threads going their own way.

"That is easily said, but how?

"This matter should not be dealt with from the outside in, but from the inside out.

"What do you mean?

"Simply, that nothing will be achieved, as long as Alvin has freedom of movement to look for the fissure where to put the knife. What you have to do is cut off any possibility of rapprochement.

"Do you think it is easy?

"I don't know, but I don't think it's impossible.

"Give me a solution.

"I have two, but first, I want you to tell me one thing. If it was just a matter of buying Long his land and no one else, would he risk that money?

"I can do it, but only once.

"In that case, please give me freedom of movement so that I can try to fix that matter. In this case, I will have to agree with my cousin in her theories regarding our conduct as lawyers.

What theories?

"He says that we are more fearsome handling the laws and the Code than a 45 colt and that we are capable of making it appear that white is black and vice versa.

"And what do you mean with that?

"That applying that theory in a different order, I am going to see if we achieve victory with arbitrary procedures up to a certain point. It will not be a very legal thing, but in this case, there are no moral laws to apply but human defense laws to put into practice. With that promise that you have made me to safeguard Long's interests at any time so that you cannot be sued, the rest does not matter.

Tell me what are you trying to do.

"Later. Let me start my way and you will know the rest in due course.

"Watch out, Gleen, I'm afraid you're overdoing it.

"Do not worry. I have a moral obligation to defend him on all grounds and I will. We will talk later.

Virginia tried to force him to expose his projects to her, but to no avail. Gleen just replied:

"I'm sorry Virginia, but lawyers have our secrets and tricks, which we only bring out in the psychological moment. I can only tell you that I am going to defend your ranch and, of course, your father's, as far as my wits and my power can go. I want to prevent you from being taken away by the devil and one day you will have to ponder whether as a lesser evil, you would not be interested in being the wife of the lawyer of an important company, with all the consequences of inconveniences that you have forged as a consequence.

"Very ironic and scathing comment, Gleen. I didn't think you were so spiteful.

"I am not, because if I were, I would not try to contribute my ingenuity to help your father and you and to overcome this obstacle. I owe you everything and I must pay somehow.

"Don't you think it's better that you take a walk around where your mother is and then go back to your studies? So far we have been able to get ahead with our own strength, which is not few.

"This is a case in which the moral force is superior to the material one. A future lawyer tells you.

"To hell with you and your laws.

And very angry, she left him, not wanting to start a too harsh dialogue with him again.

Gleen shut himself up in his uncle's office and wrote a letter, which later, riding on horseback, he went to deposit at the town post office.

The next day Long received the letter. It was a brief note, in which he was asked to report to McAlester the next day and wait at the inn in the Plaza for the visit of the buyer of his land, to finalize the cession contract there.

Long, believing in good faith that it was the ex-trafficker who was summoning him, and in view of the fact that the rancher had not sent him any notice, made his preparations to leave to be the next day in the village. As he no longer cared about the lands that were going to cease to be his hours later, he was so sorry to leave them a few hours before and he was absent to be at the place of the appointment at the appointed time.

Gleen had wandered around, glimpsing the effect of her trap, and when she saw the settler getting ready to attend the appointment, she breathed in relief.

Immediately, he returned to the ranch and looked for the foreman, asking for two or three trusted men. He expected Alvin's visit, but he did not know whether he would go alone or be accompanied by an escort and should not foolishly expose himself to a fight with superior forces.

He had to explain his trickery to the foreman. The foreman had a lot of fun meeting her and lent her three determined, well-armed men.

And with them, he moved to the settler's cabin, waiting for Alvin to show up to finalize the deal.

It was mid-afternoon when they saw the trafficker appear, accompanied by two more men. Gleen watched them advance through one of the cabin windows and ordered one of the pawns to stay with him and the other two to stand by to intervene in due course.

A little later, Alvin, confident, showed up in the fields, heading for the cabin.

His surprise was great when Gleen came out to greet him. He had the pawn at his side and outside, on both sides of Alvin and his two companions, the other two pawns were placed. Alvin looked around nervously. It smelled like a trap and he was afraid he would not get out of it.

Gleen, with an ironic accent, greeted him:

"Gee, Mr. Alvin, what a pleasant and unexpected visit. I find him much better than the last time we saw each other around here. I observe that you are a man of amazing recovery.

Alvin, trying to show cold blood and contempt, replied:

"Will you please do not disturb? I come to see Mr. Long, not you.

"To Mr. Long? Too bad you didn't come yesterday! She could have said goodbye to him before he set out on his trip to California.

"Hey, what do you say?

"That he left yesterday. We reached an agreement with him and bought his land from him. My cousin is fond of setting up an experimental exotic flower garden, and apparently this terrain lends itself well to various varieties of tropical flowers. Do you understand anything about gardening?

"Go to hell and save your jokes for whoever can stand them! I'm meeting with Mr. Long here to discuss a matter and I want to see him.

"If you think we have eaten you or we have you kidnapped, I authorize you to come in and look for you, but bear in mind that I do so on behalf of my uncle and the other owners of the basin, who are the current owners of this land. . We knew that Mr. Long wanted to sell it and together, they have acquired it, because they understood that it was worth sacrificing a handful of dollars, just to avoid having to enjoy its unpleasant neighborhood. Mr. Long signed the deed yesterday and set out on the journey without loss of time.

"That is not possible. That guy made fun of me.

"Why? You made him a proposal, he told us, we gave him a handful of dollars more and since he had not signed with another, he accepted and left. Is there something more natural?

“We are very sorry that you played this trick with very loose cards, Mr. Alvin. When we start a game and accept a stake, the least we have in our hands is good poker. And after this bad game for you, wait for us to start a different one. As you may have understood, the owners of this area are determined not to tolerate your presence or that of the oil here. Everyone has contributed to this acquisition for the purchase and this will make you understand that it is useless to try the same with someone else, because they will not sell your property for the world.

»This is the first notice; the second, I'm going to give it to him on my own. If we see you appear here again, think before trying that you are going to find a barrier of rifles ready to cut you off or leave you in the meadow so that you do not repeat the attempt. I hope you ponder it and look for oil under Death Valley or on the top of Mount Shasta, which will be easier to find than here. You have miscalculated our strengths and our unwavering resolve not to allow anyone to turn this joyful and peaceful corner of Oklahoma into hell. Get this into your head now that it's still time.

Alvin roared with fury. When he thought he had in his hands all the triumphs for the test, they had won the stake in a resounding way.

But he was one of those who would not give up as long as he had the strength to fight. He had put all his self-love into fighting Fuchs and he would keep trying.

Biting off the words, he cried out:

"Very well; You are aiming for another triumph, but some will be the last one for you and the decisive one for me. Threats do not scare me, because I can and will respond to them. Your uncle must bitterly remember the treatment he gave me when I went to propose the business.

“It is possible, but don't forget that behind“ and if necessary in front ”of my uncle, I am too.

"I celebrate it, because you and I have a pending debt to settle.

"Why don't we pay it off right now so we don't waste time? I am not one of those who tend to leave for tomorrow what I can do today.

"I do, because I do not accept anything that gives an advantage to the opposite and the advantage at this moment is theirs. There will be time for everything, because you want it or not, hell will come to the valley and black gold will spring from it, which may turn red when mixed with the blood that will flow.

"Including yours?

"Possibly including mine… and yours.

"Well, go ahead and hurry, because they are claiming me somewhere else and I want to get this matter resolved before I go.

"It will be when it has to be, but rest assured that for my part, I will not delay a single minute due to whim or hesitation.

"Congratulations. We are settled, for that day, but remember what has already happened to you once. The second will be the last.

"It will be for one of the two.

Alvin, without extreme swagger, in case Gleen lost her temper and resorted to violence, hurried away with his teammates and when he was away, Gleen, laughing with amusement at the play, ordered:

"Let's go back to the ranch, but first be careful not to leave any trace of our stay here. That when Long returns, he believes that no one visited his cabin and does not suspect what happened. Time will have to know.

CHAPTER VIII

THE FIRST EXPLOSION

Gleen, upon his arrival, understood that he should no longer hide the trick used from his uncle and Virginia and brought them together to give them an account of the success obtained.

The rancher, very serious, commented:

"That was playing dirty cards, Gleen; although I admit that the procedure was ingenious.

"Did that guy deserve better?

"I'm not talking about him, I'm talking about Long.

"There is no such dirt. For now, you will believe that Alvin was breaking his word and will have to settle. This helps us to avoid that Alvin insists on the procedure, which could be demoralizing and does not offer to buy more properties again, believing that we are all willing not to sell them. Later, if we remove the danger, you can talk to Long, explain what was done and offer him the money they gave him for his lands: If he accepts it, he will have lost nothing and if he thinks better of it and stays, everyone will have won.

"That eases my conscience and I congratulate you on your ingenuity, Gleen.

"Lawyer tricks, man. If we did not know how to take advantage of the fissures that our opponents present us, how could we triumph resoundingly? Success precisely lies in defending what seems impossible; the other, the vulgar, defends itself and has no merit.

"Well, now we need to know how Alvin will react.

"That is what we must watch. He has to do something because he is increasingly angry and will not settle for the defeats suffered.

Armor decided not to inform his neighbors of the trick used to ward off at least for the moment the attempt to open holes in those lands. It was preferable to let the matter sleep as long as possible, to avoid controversies that could provoke schism.

Armor guessed that if real danger loomed over this part of the territory, more than one would falter. Oil was poisoning not only bodies, but spirits, and many dreamed of becoming wealthy men overnight.

What he did was set up a long-distance surveillance service, to discover any surprise attempts that might arise.

Long returned two days later, puzzled and nervous. He had waited in vain for Alvin and when he was convinced that he would not appear he returned to his ranch.

And now he didn't know what to do. He was ashamed to report back to Fuchs of his failure and the ridicule he had been subjected to, although he could not explain why the interest in buying his land, and then give up on the acquisition.

The awkward time of going to report to Armor was avoided, as Gleen passed his cabin as if strolling out of distraction. Seeing Long, he stopped, saying:

"Good morning, Mr. Long. I didn't think I saw him around here yet.

"Neither am I, but... that's right. Please tell your uncle that there is nothing about the deal I told you about.

"How do you say? Did that toad repent?

"I don't know, but it seems so. He called me in McAlester to finalize the deal and I waited two days for him without showing up. That is a dirty thing that I do not tolerate to anybody.

"You can expect anything from Alvin, Mr. Long. Anyway, maybe he didn't manage to raise the money and that was it. It costs little to offer, but when it comes to giving ...

"I did not look for him, but he for me.

"Anyway, I'm not saying I'm sorry, because it wouldn't be true. For now, it is better for everyone not to disturb the tranquility that reigns here. Without that guy, this would be paradise and ... it better stay that way.

After this conversation, nothing happened. Armor's pawns were on the lookout, making discoveries, but all was still calm and it seemed that Alvin had bragged a lot about something he didn't find very easy to accomplish. There were bones that he forced to put his teeth in and this one looked like one. Several more days passed, the calm continued to reign and Gleen watched as the day of her return to school to continue her studies approached, without anything having been resolved.

And since he guessed that the tinderbox had to explode at some point, he said to his uncle:

"I am going to write to my teachers telling them that I have not fully recovered yet and that I need fifteen more days of vacation. Perhaps in that time something will happen that clears the picture.

"I think you should go, Gleen" replied the rancher. There are enough people here to face any danger.

"Yes, but I wouldn't trust all of it. After all, fifteen days or so means nothing. I can earn them by studying one more hour every day.

And it was precisely that same night that the truce was broken in a dramatic way, without anyone being able to specify how the attack had taken place. Around three in the morning and simultaneously, three fires broke out in the already dry cornfields of three settlers in the basin. When the fires were discovered, the fire, aided by a strong breeze blowing from the North, had taken on violence and threatened to devour the effort of many months of work on the land.

All that part of the valley awoke in alarm to the sharp wailing of hunting horns announcing the danger. At the Fuchs ranch, all the peonage got up quickly, ready to intervene and the rancher himself, at the head of his team, went to the affected places, which because they were quite separated from each other, forced to divide the relief forces, to be able to go everywhere.

It was a brutal and exhausting task until sunrise, without the effort being, however, very effective. At the very least, the crops were destroyed or almost destroyed, although it was possible to prevent the cabins, some sheds and certain other elements, from being burned.

Consternation reigned among the owners of the valley. Alvin had begun to strike with the force that the elements involved in the oil gave him and was beginning to undermine, not only the resistance and strength of his enemies, but their morale.

What he had not achieved by persuasion and offering, he sought to achieve by destruction and fear, and Fuchs began to fear that at the last minute, the triumph would be his enemy.

When the fires were extinguished, when those three pictures of ruin and misery were contemplated in the sunlight, the faces of all were contracted and rigid, making out the storms that were undermining the injured.

Until one, stepping forward, exclaimed:

"Here is what we have achieved with all this, Mr. Fuchs and it is necessary to tell you, since you have been the one who painted the situation in a different way and forced us to commit ourselves to something that has been the undoing of some.

"I don't know whether or not there will be oil in these damn lands, but we would have gained more by allowing them to check it. Had they failed, now we would be calm and these stupid ruins would have been avoided and if they had really taken oil who knows the path that our situation would have taken at this time ... even if you didn't like it.

Fuchs, faced with the settler's aggressive tirade, replied:

"It is possible, but stop pondering what would have happened to those who, unfortunately, had not been lucky enough to find black gold on their properties.

"Anything worse than this? "Cried the settler, pointing desperately to his charred ears." No, not worse, because at least what we had would have remained intact.

"You believe? Do you know anything about the influence of oil on land and crops? But if it is a poison that scorches everything and kills it.

"Very well, but ruin by ruin, the other was preferable, because at least the favored would have made use of the bowels of their crops. No, this cannot go on like this and will not go on. The commitments are over when, despite them, no one has been able to protect our modest estates. Today the blow has been given to three, tomorrow it can be given to others and end up plunging us all into ruin. Perhaps not to you, because you have many men to defend your property, but what do we gain from your saving what is yours, if we lose what is ours? I am broke, sunk, in misery, but unless ... I will see if I save myself in some way. What I have not let others do on my land, I will do myself. I am going to open holes in it until I cross the globe from part to part and as that coveted oil sprouts,

The other two victims, upon hearing him, exclaimed with fierce accents:

"That's right and it will. We will do the same and I make a proposal to you two. What may arise in any of our lands, to third parts of utility and if it sprouts in all three, the better.

Fuchs, faced with the terrible threat that ruined all his efforts to defend his pastures from the terrible and deadly influence of oil, lost control of his nerves, and standing up menacingly, he bellowed:

"Listen; This has become a hell of conflicting interests, in which, apparently, we will all have to fight to defend what is ours. I looked for the most loyal way so that no one would be harmed and it is not my fault that certain ruffians, appealing to miserable sabotage, have committed these scoundrels that have no qualification.

But just as you talk about defending what is yours, I have to warn that I will defend what is mine. Oil is a threat to several miles of pasture and to a few thousand horns that has taken me several years and many efforts to achieve. I came here to fight with the earth, with the elements and with the undesirables, to achieve what I now possess and I had to risk my life many times to defend and preserve it. If now someone, whoever he is, threatens again what it cost me so much sacrifice to raise, he will be my enemy and as such I will treat him.

»Oil is not real gold. Extracting this does not harm a third party. Getting oil out of a well is poison for the others around it and I cannot tolerate that anyone undoes my finances from me. I want to warn you, because if that way they declare war on me, I will accept it against anyone, however painful it may be for me to turn against my friends until today and whom I in good faith tried to defend.

"Don't talk nonsense" bellowed one. If it had been convenient for you to extract oil from your pastures, you would not have waited for them to come and propose it, you would have looked for it on your own, without thinking of others, because within your property you could do whatever you wanted. win. Well, that happens to us; within our plots we can do what we want and no one will be able to prevent it.

" Me! Fuchs bellowed.

"You.

"If I; because it can harm me and just as I have not wanted to harm others by trying first, I will not tolerate anyone ruining me. I want to warn that I will put all my men in motion and that the first one to be caught opening a hole, before he gets to open it completely, they will put one on his head with an ounce of lead and it will all be over.

A dramatic silence welcomed the threat. Fuchs had Gleen and several of his team's pawns by his side, and they seemed ready to fight back.

"So why don't you compensate us for the damage suffered as it comes from you? "Said a settler.

"I would like to, but I couldn't make it up to everyone. What I can do is help them not to go hungry for the moment and later, when this is resolved, because it has to be resolved and perhaps not taking long, then we will study how to alleviate these losses.

"Words and nothing but words. The practical is another thing and if there is oil here ... that is the practical.

"I hope you think about it well," warned Fuchs.

"It is meditated" bellowed one; I'm in charge of my house and I'll do whatever I want. The others who follow the path that they deem most convenient for them.

Disorientation reigned among the assembled. Those who had not yet suffered attacks or losses did not dare to join the victims, but they stood by the expectation, because if the others defied the threats of Fuchs and found oil, they would all start digging in their lands looking like wild beasts. of new and fruitful wells.

Armor asked a general question:

What do others think?

No one seemed willing to take the initiative, until one replied:

"For the moment, we reserve our opinion. Circumstances rule and we will temper ourselves with them.

The answer was ambiguous, but threatening, because if someone discovered oil, others, like wild beasts, would go looking for it too.

The rancher was beside himself. He knew he was cornered and he could not manage to dominate so many hostile elements in essence or power.

And fearing to provoke the cataclysm, he decided to cut off such a dramatic situation, saying:

"Sirs, I have said my last word. If as someone has indicated, the time has come to save themselves who can and each one goes to his own, and not to the general interest, I will defend what is mine tooth and nail and without looking against whom. I will sacrifice my life if necessary to prevent my pastures from turning into a gray desert and my cattle from being poisoned. Following the theory of some, I do what others do: defend what is mine. For this reason, I repeat that whoever makes a single drop of oil sprout and leads me to ruin ... must prepare, because I kill him.

And followed by his own, he left the meeting to return to the ranch.

The situation had become dire. Death began to walk his scythe through the valley, wondering what his first and best prey would be and everyone knew they were threatened by his scythe at any moment. The three victims could carry out their threat to open wells, but they could not ignore Fuchs's, who would comply with the valuable help of his pawns. These, first of all, were cowboys and defended the pastures and cattle on which their lives depended.

They would back Fuchs aggressively and there were a lot of them. Only by organizing a force to oppose their own could they defy that terrible threat.

What was going to happen from then on? Nobody could predict it, but everyone was convinced that it would be something too tragic for some.

Fuchs's threat shocked the three settlers whose ruin had so tragically been accomplished, and before challenging the rancher's power, they exchanged views. And there was someone who proposed:

"I think the best thing is to go to McAlester, get in touch with the Oklahoma Oil Company, explain the case to them, and have them send men in sufficient numbers to open the holes. If they have brought about our downfall, let them also expose something to move forward in their endeavor. We will demand an amount from them for the rental of the parcels and at least, as long as it is known whether or not there is oil, we will recover some of what was lost.

One of them was appointed so that without loss of time he could carry out the management that interested them so much.

The settler showed up at the town, precisely at the time when Alvin was there exchanging impressions with the director. He had gotten his share to be bought in the wells he had discovered and awaited the result of the sabotage that he himself had organized, to sow tares among the owners of the basin and break the pact signed between them. He was enraged by what he believed to be Long's bad job, and in the face of so much resistance and difficulty moving forward, he hadn't hesitated to resort to drastic procedures.

Gleen's threats hadn't impressed him, because now, with money, he could buy consciences and well-armed hands to get the job done.

The manager, who was aware of Alvin's stubborn struggle with the Wesley Valley landowners, was quick to call the former dealer to listen to the settler and hear his propositions.

The settler, being introduced to Alvin, advanced on him furiously, roaring:

"Have you been the scoundrel who ...?

"Calm down, friend, and don't rise up before your time. They just told me that you are coming to offer the company your properties to try to open wells and if so, we can understand each other well.

"I would not have appealed to such procedures, if Fuchs, who has had you in his fist, had not forced me to do so. I have simply tried to lease land to whoever wanted to to start the search; something that would have benefited everyone, if there was oil there, as we suppose, but Fuchs treated me badly, threatened me, even mistreated me and objected without any right to others doing what he said he was not interested in.

And I have had to respond in the same way. I have made a matter of self-esteem to discover oil there, if there is any, and I appealed to the measures that they left me at hand. I'm sorry you were unlucky, but we will try to fix that, if you are really willing to allow wells to be dug.

"Of course we are willing and we would have done it ourselves, if Fuchs hadn't threatened us with shooting him out. We have broken all relations with him, but the three of us cannot stand in front of his team, that is why we have come to offer the Company the land so that it, if it has enough men, can send the necessary ones to dig wells, if it is offered to us. compensation for damages suffered.

Alvin, who was bursting with joy at knowing that he was about to carry out his threats, replied:

"I am willing to pay you the value of what was lost in the fires and later, if we discover oil, we will reach an agreement, either by buying the land from you, or by offering you a share in the product of each well that is opened with gasoline.

"In that case, I have authorization from my colleagues to deal with you about the lease. As soon as the value of the lost is paid to us, we will allow entry there.

"Perfectly. We will try to assess those losses and sign the document.

They were in an office discussing the money to be delivered and the conditions of the contract, until they reached an agreement.

The settler signed on behalf of the three, received the money and said:

"When do you plan to send your people?

"The day after tomorrow I will send forty men with the necessary equipment so that the work can be carried out sooner and in better conditions.

"Very well, but don't forget that Fuchs has all his pawns on alarm and that they are guarding the prairie to prevent any intrusion into our lands.

"It is the same to me. Now that I know I have the right to go in there and maneuver with absolute freedom. I promise you, Fuchs will remember the day he dared to defy me in such an idiotic way.

»You can go back to your lands and reassure your companions by giving them your money. In two days we will talk.

The settler returned to his destroyed fields and that same night, he met with the other two victims. They felt reassured after receiving their money. From then on, let Fuchs deal with his enemy.

Both Armor and his nephew were feeling very nervous. They knew that the terrible storm would soon break out and they feared its consequences, because it hurt them to have to face not only their enemy, but their own neighbors.

But two days later, one of the pawns who watched from a distance, galloped back to announce to Fuchs, that two enormous loaded carts did not know what, because the awnings hid the cargo and a large group of horsemen, advanced from the North with direction to that part of the valley.

Fuchs guessed it was Alvin. He kept his promise to accept the battle and provoked it, because without provoking it he could achieve nothing.

This made him understand that it would be useless to appeal to the help of those who until very recently had been his allies. All he could hope for was for them to be neutral as long as they had no reason to bow to one side or the other.

The stakes were high and Armor set out to fight the battle. Maybe if he won it, he would put the danger away forever.

He harassed his peons and they prepared to repel the intruders who tried to penetrate the colonists' lands.

But his astonishment and anger were enormous, when two horsemen stood out from the group, on whose chests the silver stars of sheriffs or commissioners, at least, shone in the sun.

One was McAlester's deputy sheriff and the other a McAlester sheriff.

The deputy sheriff advanced toward the hostile group of Fuchs and his pawns, and the rancher, fearing the worst, ordered his men to keep their hands to themselves.

"Which one of you is Armor Fuchs?

"I" replied the rancher hoarsely saluting the deputy sheriff.

"Very well, in this case, I have to communicate something to you from my boss, the sheriff general of this basin. These men who precede me, come in use of their perfect right to take possession of land that they have leased, according to documents that they duly exhibited and in which they plan to work in drilling operations to search for oil.

»As apparently, according to the landlord's complaint, you oppose with the threat of force that they use that right that protects the Law, I come on behalf of the sheriff to give you the notice and to warn you that any attempt of attack or coercion to prevent them Exercising that perfect right that assists them will affect you and whoever supports you in an aggressive action.

»And if this occurs and the legitimate right of defense on the part of the attacked person is adverse to him, apart from the legal responsibilities required by law, nothing shall reproach or demand accountability from those who, defending his own, could cause serious losses to the contrary. . I hope you take notice and withdraw your forces to your ranch. Leaving others free to use their rights.

Fuchs, who was livid, replied, biting the words:

"And who assures me against the serious dangers that the use of that right that the law protects will cause me?

"What does it mean?

"You know it. As oil sprouts and runs through the fields, dries the grass, burns it, destroys the sap that it contains and devastates everything around it. I have flourishing pastures and a few thousand head of cattle that can be poisoned if the oil rises and as it is safe, it destroys my pastures. Who preserves me from this damage?

»I don't care what the neighbor does if it doesn't harm me, but if in order for him to get rich I have to ruin myself, that I will not tolerate with the law and against the law.

"If so, you can file a claim for damages and have the courts rule if there were any and how much. The law is the law and it must be respected.

"Do you think that is safe and positive? Do you think that they would pay me the many thousands of dollars that all this is worth, and the yield that I extract from it per year? Do you think that in order to favor others, I have to give up what is mine in any case? Why don't they look for oil in the open grasslands in the deserts, or on the slopes of the mountains where they can harm no one? Why should it be precisely in a nucleus of fertile land, in which everything that the life of the peoples needs to feed themselves is produced? Is it that with this excessive and crazy ambition that has shaken people to look for oil as if that damned liquid constituted everything, the fatal reduction or the death of livestock and agriculture can be allowed, as much or even more necessary than oil? Why not harmonize the two without harming one another?

"You propose to me a theory that corresponds to the governments and not to me to solve it. I represent the law to dry and the law protects those who have requested protection from it, the rest can be raised by whoever corresponds to seek that solution that I do not deny.

"Of course, and when that is studied and solved in fifty years, where will the losers be?

"I am sorry that I cannot solve your problems, but it is not in my power. My mission is one and I fulfill it; the rest to be resolved by whoever has the authority and power to do so.

Fuchs, about to explode, bellowed:

"Very well, these people have the right to settle in those lands and open holes to bury everyone. Let them open them until they come out on the other side of the Earth and as long as they limit themselves to that, I will limit myself to waiting, but if they have the misfortune to make oil come out, and it threatens my lands, then hell is going to seem to some a place of recreation with which he is going to explode here. I have sworn that before seeing my burned lands and my carcasses, they will have to kill me and that they prepare to try, but as long as they do not succeed, let them fear for their oil, for their lives and for the globe. It's all I have to tell you.

And without waiting for more, he gestured to his men and the team, tense, with teeth clenched by the badly contained fury, returned to the ranch, while the two large wagons with their cargo and the large picket of defenders guarding them. , they went ahead, preceded by the deputy sheriff and the commissioner, as a guarantee that no one would prevent them from reaching the leased lands and settling on them. The rest, what might be derived from that daring act, could only be predicted by fate.

CHAPTER IX

PETROLEUM! PETROLEUM!

Overjoyed at his success, Alvin advanced with this huge machine towards the lands of the three settlers. He had known how to do things with skill, hiding himself in the aid of authority. He knew it was a momentary brake on Fuchs's aggressive impulse, a parenthesis that would allow him without fight and exposure to reach the lands with his men and equipment intact, but he was no longer so sure that the moral protection of the law would serve him. much if the oil came to gush out.

Then, it would be the force that would say its last word, but even so, in case of locating oil, since the find was well worth exposing much and spending more, it would hire men in sufficient numbers to beat its hated rival.

So far he had enough to protect the preliminary soundings; later, luck would have its last word. The two large carts carried the most precise material for the first attempts. It was electronic equipment, many hundreds of yards of cables, a small drilling rig, and dynamite in abundance. The preliminary work would consist of opening holes, exploding the dynamite charge in them and studying the reverberations of the booms with the seismographs, listening to the ground and drawing up maps, which would be used for the study of the technicians until the domes were located.

But sometimes, all these scientific works were useless in one sense or another. Useless, if there was no oil in the place where it was sought and useless if luck made them prepare to delve into favorable places where luck had led them to discover oil almost to the ground, because then, it was enough to chop a few meters by introducing a simple hollow tube through the hole, so that when it reached the gap where the oil was, it would gush out with the force of a projectile, saving studies, maps and other technical data that lavish nature made superfluous.

The arrival of that material and of so many men to protect it, put the rest of the landowners in that part in shock. Apparently, the material was not yet complete; New wagons were yet to arrive with more drilling rigs and drill pipes, and a nervous and feverish restlessness seized everyone.

What would happen if oil emerged on the lands of those three determined settlers? Why couldn't the others also try their luck if the oil craze had already taken hold of everyone and if it exploded, the face of the valley would change as if it had been shaken by geological chaos? The interesting thing was that everyone tried their luck at the same time. If there was for everyone, nothing to waste time and if there was not, everyone would be convinced at the same time as how sterile the terrain is.

For this reason, as soon as the drilling preparations began in the lands of the settlers affected by the fire, in all the other places they began as a test, with no effective means other than picks, shovels and some hollow iron bars, the attempt of looking for possible oil, all dreaming of finding it as soon as they scratched the ground.

At the Fuchs ranch, tension reigned. The rancher, excited, only spoke of a terrible fight without quarter and there was no way to calm his nerves.

Virginia was frightened by her father's attitude; Twice he had tried to leave the farm alone, obsessed with finding Alvin to finish him off, and Gleen, who was perfectly aware of everything, tried to calm him down, saying:

"Listen, man; We gain nothing by losing control of our nerves and anticipating events. No one is sure that what they are looking for can exist and as long as oil does not emerge, why despair and provoke something that could be fatal?

If they did not find it, there would be nothing to try and failure and loss would be for them. Perhaps then they will realize their madness and regret having been carried away by the fantasy.

»If this happens, there will be no need to fight and expose lives uselessly. Everything will sink on its own, without adding fuel to the fire.

"This is all very sensible in theory, Gleen; But what if it arises, who avoids the catastrophe then? What I want is to anticipate what would later be irremediable.

"I understand you, but do you really think that you would avoid it by provoking that fight? Note that Alvin has not come unprepared this time; He brings with him forty well-armed men, who will undoubtedly be ready to fight, if it were not more than that, our team, although a little less numerous, could perhaps try to sweep those people away, but have you thought about the help they would give Alvin the other owners, when they have been influenced by the oil madness and all have turned the valley into a hell where there is no arm that at this moment does not grasp the peaks to delve into the earth? They would join Alvin's men and form a contingent against whom we could do nothing for quantity, even if not for quality.

"So what do you think I should do, allow them to turn my pastures into a field of desolation?

"Could you somehow prevent it, if that has to happen? I think not, and to launch into a desperate fight, there is always time, especially if there is a serious moment to try.

»I am not saying this because I am afraid to be one more in the fight; On the contrary, I have pending with Alvin the balance of a fight and I will not leave here without measuring myself with him, but in a definitive way.

"So keep in mind that if you have to fight, I will be by your side at the decisive moment. I only understand that the fight, or should never be raised for lack of a basic reason, or when it occurs, that it is for something to life or death.

The rancher did not seem to be convinced by the appeals that his calm towards the young man, but Virginia, who feared for her father's life, supported Gleen and with him fought morally to convince Fuchs.

He ended up calming down a bit and promising sanity. He must cling to the last hope he had; the one that the attempts failed and they did not find oil.

But from that moment on, his nerves would suffer jolts capable of driving him mad, every time the wind carried the echo of the explosions of dynamite to the farm, widening and deepening the holes that were opening.

Gleen was concerned. He knew what might flare up at some point and didn't see a viable solution to the potential drama.

Oil, rushing through the furrows on other people's land, could be Fuchs's undoing, without benefit, but why, if the pastures were threatened, couldn't this ruin be mitigated with a counterpart?

If there was oil in the valley, it could just as well come from Long's lands, or anybody else, as it could from Fuchs's own pastures, and if this had to happen, why not get ahead of the rest, looking right there for what? what could be everywhere?

Pasture and cattle could be lost, but if the land contained oil, it would compensate for the loss with its value, and ultimately, the sale of the fields would compensate the rancher for his losses.

But, this logical reasoning, who exposed it to Armor? In their obsession, they would have rejected him furiously without wanting to hear about him.

And yet it was a prudent and farsighted measure, not to be overlooked. When you have to face big events, the solutions cannot be coupled with your desire, but with what can be extracted from those same events, losing the least and gaining the most.

Harassed by this idea, he made Virginia share in it. The girl was not stupid; Gleen knew too much logic to expose reality without false appearances, and she made it known to her cousin.

This, convinced by their arguments, replied:

"I think like you, Gleen; If it is inevitable that oil arises and it can ruin us for the benefit only of others, why not remedy our ruin with the same thing that produces it for us? In spite of my father, reality will only be one and whether he likes oil or not, it would be the stupid kind to ruin us and give up what could be our salvation.

"But I think like you, who exposes this to him? It wouldn't be me, despite all the reasons.

"Neither do I, but, nevertheless, there are many ways to overcome certain difficulties.

"How?

"I have an idea, and I am going to ask you to give your opinion on it, so that, ultimately, the responsibility lies with everyone. You have a foreman who is a very sensible man. I would dare to explain all this to him, to see what his opinion is, and if he thinks like us, then, according to him, we could try something without your father finding out, at least for now.

»The idea is, that looking for a place of the most remote and hidden of the pastures, where it is difficult to pass through there, a couple of men would dedicate themselves to dig as much as possible, in search of a possible well. There are long iron tubes in the sheds, which are used to replace the pieces of pipe that join the ponds. With them, they could try an essay, although I know it would not be very scientific, but, who knows, at least it would be an initiation of what others do, and if any of the others are lucky in that sense, why not accept that here it was also had?

There is no other solution, Virginia. Either the failure is resounding, or we all drown in oil; but yes, that we are all and not just a few.

»Fortune by fortune; If the cattle ranch is lost, the oil comes up and, later ... well, with what it yields, you can start all over again, even if there is a need to leave this damned land and go to Texas, or where cattle are guaranteed not to be poisoned by oil.

"Your idea is good, Gleen, but... what if my father finds out?

"If he finds out ahead of time, all that can happen is he will forbid further digging. I will take responsibility for the idea and let it be what God wants.

"As things have become, it is suicidal to go against the current, and what is imposed is to swim in favor of it.

Virginia ended up agreeing and promised Gleen to speak with the foreman and present the idea to him.

The foreman thought deeply before answering, and finally said:

"I think the best solution may be that. I know that the boss will not like it, because he is obsessed with not knowing anything about oil, but if it is ever going to flow and it has to destroy this, at least he should have compensation. What you lose on the one hand, you win on the other, and then, if you want, we will go somewhere else to establish a new ranch, where we are not threatened by that hell.

"Therefore, I am going to second your idea. I think there is a very good place to try it, because if we find oil in it, we have a deep ravine next to it, which could serve as a natural raft to collect it, without losing a drop, until someone takes care of bottling it and removing it from there. Once things are done, let them be done with the head.

"Magnificent! Gleen exclaimed. Do you want us to go see that place?

"Let's go there.

The visit convinced both young men of the reason that he was assisting the foreman. Digging in that site, which was also protected by wild hedges, which would hide those who acted in it, should oil arise, it could descend through a crevice widened for that purpose and pour into a long and deep ravine that opened lower than that ground, at a distance of twenty yards.

In agreement, the foreman agreed with them to choose a couple of trusted men and dedicate them to this work, after an explanation of the reason for that attempt. Like good cowboys, they also hated oil, and would not do such a job by their own pleasure.

Everyone had to take care that Fuchs did not find out about the maneuver, so they could not use dynamite to dig the holes, because they would report themselves and Fuchs would fly into a rage against the conspirators. And once this matter was resolved, everyone was waiting for what might come up.

No one was unaware that they had under their feet a terrible and dilated barrel of gunpowder that could tragically explode from one moment to another, and that the paradoxical fuse that would make it fly would be the first black oil spout to emerge from their entrails.

A deadly week had passed since Alvin had arrived in his gear, and although the fever of madness was working everywhere, the situation remained stationary.

Dozens of shallow wells had been started, filling them with dynamite, which when exploded enlarged the holes, but the signs of oil were nowhere to be found.

Alvin wasn't feeling hopeless yet. He was practicing what that was, he had dug enough holes to no avail, at least at certain depths, but this had helped the technicians study the terrain, vibrations, and other technical aspects of the difficult problem.

And he knew of wells that had consumed weeks and even months, some to be sterile and others, to, ultimately, provide the desired product, tenacity and expense put at the service of that insecure business.

But some of those who, infected with this fever, had tried to search on their own with much less practical means than Alvin, were beginning to feel hopeless. They had been hallucinated from the first intention, believing that this was something very easy and fast and they watched with concern how the days passed, they used their energies in that enormous work and the result was negative, with double damage for them, because the rest of their Work, until then practical and rewarding, had abandoned him, exposing himself to losing both.

Within two weeks of the start of the work, the least patient had thrown their picks and shovels in dismay and were gazing furiously at the deep, dry, sterile pits and the huge piles of earth piled up on the sides, occupying a space, which dedicated to something else, it would have given more performance.

And sulking and crestfallen, they sought each other to exchange impressions and encourage each other, if this was possible.

"What do you think? "Asked one." We have been wasting energy and wasting time for more than two weeks, and there is no sign of anything. Do you think that, at last, we will achieve something?

"Who knows? "Answered another, hoarsely." I have abandoned my fields that needed my attention more than ever and I am like you. I begin to believe that we have done a crazy thing to let ourselves be seduced by the tenacity of that guy who has revolutionized us all.

"That seems to me" affirmed a third party. Fuchs assured us many times that everything was born out of a personal antagonism between him and that man. We will end up having to agree with him, and how is he going to laugh at us if he is the only one who has seen clearly.

"Still nothing can be said" assured another, who still hoped to achieve his ambition. Brown has told me that this Alvin is not disappointed, and that his men are still working hard. He assures that, at times, holes have been dug that have taken two and three months to make the oil gush.

"Well, it is possible, but ... who can be digging for three months and without means like him? If so, it would take us a year and a half to reach that depth.

"I think so" answered the first "and I think that we have been foolish by launching ourselves to search on our own. If there is oil and that guy brings it out, he will be interested in continuing to drill wells, and it is he who must deal with us to open others on our properties.

"But if he does it, he'll want more of it.

"It is natural, but if by not giving it, we cannot make it sprout, think that all the stored liquid will come out of your wells and we will have lost our part.

"That's true. We will have to depend on him

"But if" another "was not found and that guy has to go with his impedimenta elsewhere, he will not have lost more than the money he used, of course, but we, in what situation will we be left? We have stood up to Mr Fuchs, and from now on our relations will be less than cordial. He's furious about everything that happened and won't want to hear from us.

"Well, there he" affirmed one. " Until now, I have only lived on what my property gives me.

"And all of them, but sometimes... our troubles have forced us to turn to him, and he always lent us a hand. I don't think after this, I will.

"Yes, you never know how to get it right.

"It's a shame" commented another ", because if there is a lot of oil here, have you stopped to think about the benefit we would get in a short time? Just selling our land to the Company would give us twenty times what it's worth now, and it's worth the gamble, if there's a chance of winning that way.

"That will have to be seen. As it takes a long time to find something, we will all end up broke or something similar.

But Alvin was not worried about the discouragements of the other owners. He knew what that was and he didn't get discouraged so soon, although he was already starting to get nervous, because if he failed, apart from the ridiculous running, he would have wasted a large part of what he had just collected for the sold wells and his revenge on Fuchs I would be disappointed.

But he still had hope. The engineer who had accompanied him and his assistants, constantly studied the characteristics of the explosions, examined the extracted earth and were pending of their work.

Days later, Alvin trembled with emotion, when through the hollow tube that sank into the earth, he perceived a strange smell, which until then he had not perceived. It was like a very faint smell of petroleum far away, but a smell nonetheless.

He consulted with the engineer, who told him:

"It is very possible that it is a precursor gas for the well burst. If so, I'm afraid you don't have the ground ready to pick it up immediately. A lot of oil is going to be lost.

And Alvin, with a fierce accent, said:

"I have foreseen it and I don't care; rather, my wish is for it to be a large expansion well, expelling many gallons of oil per minute.

"To lose more money?

"To invade this land in one day and descend these slopes. Do you see down there, that hawthorn fence? Well, it is the one that separates the pastures from the man I hate the most in the world and the one who hates me the most. If I tell you that I have come here to risk my money and even my life to give me the pleasure of seeing the oil gush out and descend like a waterfall towards your pastures only to wash them away and turn them into a ruin, I am not lying to you. This is my greatest pleasure and, to achieve it, I would give all that may be of use to me in any nascent well.

"Well, if so, I suspect that his revenge is close to consummating. What remains to be known is what the "beneficiary's" reaction will be.

"I suppose her, and I'm prepared for her, that's why I have forty men here paying them a good salary for doing nothing so far. They have the mission of receiving the wave of rage from my enemy and I hope that if he decides to strike back at me, he will receive the last and the most fatal for him.

The news that symptoms of gas were beginning to appear from the main well that was being opened spread like wildfire throughout the properties. Finally, it seemed that the projects of the stubborn wildcatter were going to be a reality and that oil was going to emerge as a promise, which could reach not just one, but many.

And again, the fever to keep exploring invaded everyone. Those who had left the peaks to return to tend their crops, forgot these to take up the weapons of work again, and a fever of madness spread from end to end in the valley.

Everyone guessed that the outbreak was near and that at some point, what for some was already an entelechy, would become reality.

Such was the fever that the search journey was spliced at night. Kerosene lamps fantastically illuminated the workplaces, where one and the other, according to their means, were biting hard.

And it was approximately three in the morning, when in the well where Alvin had placed his hopes, the oil surged powerful, brave. Through the hollow and thick tube of the drilling tower, the enormous jet arose, reaching a height of dozen and a half yards, and later, having lost the force of expansion, it descended in a black and pestilential jet, which caught the various workers who They worked drilling and he disguised them by turning them into black ghosts dripping with foul liquid.

A huge shout of joy erupted from dozens of throats at the long-awaited find, and as the liquid continued to surge into the black space of night, in an uninterrupted stream. Throats were hoarse, screaming:

"Petroleum! Petroleum!

And the screams, carried by the wind, reached Fuchs's ranch, like a war bugle.

The hour of the battle had sounded and there would be no human power that could stop it for a single moment.

CHAPTER X

FIRE IN HELL

The light of the new day allowed the landscape to be registered. Fuchs, who was livid with anger, looked longingly off into the distance. In the reddish morning light, the spout of the cursed oil was like a black parable, staining the clarity of the landscape and the dirty liquid, lacking adequate places to be collected, had formed various furrows, like poisoned snakes descending through the river. sloping terrain and looking down the pastures of Fuchs, to enter them.

And the rancher, realizing that the catastrophe was already inevitable, began to roar like a madman:

"My men to me, we must sweep away those bastards who have cowardly brought us ruin! Go ahead!

The peons, enraged, prepared their horses ready to launch themselves into the fight, and Virginia, terrified, wanted to stop her father, but he, abruptly, rejected her, to launch blindly towards the place where the oil continued to flow and feed the streams, that had already started seeping through the hawthorn fence.

Gleen, noticing his uncle's state of mind, could do nothing but jump onto the horse and try to follow the rancher, to protect him to the best of his ability.

He knew that there was no human power to stop him in his eagerness to fight and win or die.

The team, infected with the same fury as their employer, since they too were affected by the possible ruin of the ranch, had rushed to request their mounts and weapons and were preparing to fight the hard battle. Like an avalanche, they left the pastures and launched impetuously towards the place where the oil was gushing, ready to destroy whatever they found in their path.

Alvin, who had foreseen the fierce reaction of his enemy, had his men prepared for the clash, and thus, as soon as they realized that the team was upon them, their guards rushed out to meet them to cut them off and not allow them to approach the well.

Soon that piece of the valley became a terrible battlefield. They had been quick to disintegrate so as not to form a compact mass, easy to concentrate the shots against it, and they were looking for each other with savage fury, ready to annihilate each other.

The rifles were the first to sing their song of death, firing from a distance, but when the momentum of the horses cut ground and they charged, the rifles were annoying and impractical weapons, so they were quickly replaced by the "Colt »Easier to use and more practical for an almost hand-to-hand fight.

The settlers, terrified by the tragic picture that was offered to their eyes, fled the battlefield, seeking refuge in their huts or crushing themselves among the fields to steal the body to the gale of projectiles that hissed sinisterly around them.

Alvin, spurred on by his hatred for Fuchs and fearing that the desperate thrust of his men might overwhelm his own, wiping out what so much effort and money had cost him to achieve, did not sit idly by. He was not a coward, he was encouraged by a violent hatred against his enemy and he understood that he should be one more to join the fight and set an example so that others would not feel some faintness that could be fatal to them.

And as one more he threw his horse into the maelstrom of the fight, looking for the rancher among the bustle of the team members. If he had to expose himself, he wanted to do it by personally searching for his rival.

Fuchs, animated by the same homicidal sentiment, was also looking for him, but there was something else that obsessed him and that had become the main target of his attack.

When he left the ranch, he had furiously uprooted some clumps of resinous plants, which he lit on the saddle without hardly stopping in this work. Green watched him and wanted to ask him uneasily what he was up to, but the rancher, ignoring him, continued to gallop frantically and the young man gave up, limiting himself to following him, as if he were his shadow, fearing any tragic excess of the exalted rancher, who had lost control of his reasoning and was animated only by a terrible idea: that of destroying everything that stood in his way.

And Gleen felt more and more oppressed as he watched his uncle gallop straight toward the erect tower, stuck in the fields of one of the settlers, from whose dome the thick spout of the spout still sprouted, black and foul.

What was it up to? Restlessness overcame him and he tried to resist her advance. In this part, a dozen guards had gathered, determined not to allow their enemies to reach the well.

The team foreman had also noticed the straight path of his patron, he hastened to maneuver so as not to be separated from him and dragged three more men after him, all of whom made up a small group isolated from the rest of the fighters.

The guardians of the well hurried to close the distance, coming out in front of the rancher, to prevent him from reaching the well, but Fuchs's hands were two volcanoes of death, handling the two "Colts" with which he was provided.

His followers also handled double the number of weapons that the current one, and thus, each man fired by two and doubled his attack and defense strength.

For a few minutes, both sides seemed stopped by the force of the collision. The revolvers worked to sow death and terror, and four of the guards fell from their horses, while two of Fuchs' pawns leaned over their mounts, receiving the hallucinatory caress of the bullets.

But the rancher's momentum was overwhelming, seconded by the foreman and his nephew. Two new enemies were well hit, and the others were forced to retreat, pursued by the attackers.

But, suddenly, the rancher was delayed, he pulled the thick bundle of resinous branches that hung from the saddle and, taking out a match, set it on fire.

The resin began to burn and the branches threatened to become a small fire in the hands of the rancher, who, blind with fury, without measuring the danger, galloped swiftly in the direction of the well.

Gleen, realizing that he had fallen behind, turned his head in search of him, and discovering him with the burning branches in his hands, guessed the madness he intended to commit, and, terrified, roared:

"Uncle! Uncle! Back ... no, not that ... by all the saints! James ... help me hold him back!

And it was impossible to reach him before he finished his terrible and dramatic work. Blindly, he advanced towards the high spout, and when he came to a place that he thought could throw the burning branches, he jerked his arm with terrible courage and threw them into the flammable liquid that formed a small raft when it fell.

Immediately, he tried to back away, but did not have time. The gases of that terrible flammable mass expanded in the explosion. The rancher and his mount, caught in the explosive cone, were thrown like projectiles, and Gleen, like the foreman, watched with terror as both bodies were projected in front of them, almost overwhelming them when they were thrown to go to fall half destroyed to enough yards away.

Gleen and the foreman had providentially spared the same horrific death as the rancher because of their delay in reaching him, but still they suffered from the suffocating heat of the enormous heat wave that swept through when the fire broke out.

And immediately, something dantesque took place, which made everyone's hair stand on end, because that was something never contemplated.

Now, no longer a black mass rose from the tower of the well, but a continuous stream of flames, that poured on the ground. The fire, by running fast, had followed the furrows full of oil, spreading the fire along the land, towards the ranch where the extracted oil was already seeping and as a complement, the flames, as they spread, had embraced each other. the dry grass of the grassy lands, to the ears about to be cut from the fields, and, the landscape had become a fierce inferno of flames, which spread from one side to the other, devouring fields, fields, sheds, barracks , tools and how much the voracious element was finding in its path.

The terrified combatants had stopped fighting, aware of the danger that loomed over them and against which they could not fight. Furthermore, the fire, by running without fixation from one place to another, threatening to envelop them inside its fire, forced them to retreat, to escape from that hell that would end up devouring them with its insatiable desire for destruction.

Gleen, terrified, just a little recovered from the barbaric shock, hastened to gallop towards the place where Fuchs and his horse had been left on the ground, unrecognizable, and getting off, ran towards the destroyed body of his uncle, being helped by the foreman, who was livid and contracted with the terrible shock suffered.

For his part, Alvin, who was fighting not far from the scene of the terrible catastrophe, being surprised by the rancher's suicidal maneuver, issued a terrible oath, and with his face contorted by an ignoble grimace of concentrated anger, he launched his horse forward, looking for the rancher to quench in him all the poisonous anger that devoured his soul with more force than the fire that began to devour everything within its reach.

And he was almost on top of Gleen and the foreman as they tried to lift Fuchs's body, to carry it away and prevent the fire from taking hold of it.

Gleen barely had time to notice the impetuous and desperate advance of Alvin, who, revolver in hand, threw his horse over the group, firing out of control.

The young man, in a desperate movement, seized the revolver that he had left next to him as he leaned over his uncle's body, and fired at Alvin, when he did in turn when he recognized him.

Gleen had only two bullets in the barrel of the revolver, and both of them were eagerly directed at the ex-dealer's body as he leaned sideways on his horse to fire as well.

Alvin gave a mind-boggling roar of pain and turned completely on his side, and fell to the ground, where he took two tragic turns to shrink, while Gleen felt the pull of one of his opponent's bullets, brushing against his left arm.

But, fortunately, his wound was not serious, while the two that Alvin had received were mortal of necessity.

The denouement was so quick that when the foreman wanted to intervene, everything was over.

But there was no time to comment. The fire advanced everywhere, and Gleen, fearing to be in the devouring spotlight, cried out:

"Soon, James, take that vulture's horse! You have to put my uncle's body in it and get out of here before it's too late. Poor Virginia, when on the ruin on her heels, she learns of the tragic death of her father.

The half-destroyed corpse was crossed in the saddle of Alvin's horse, leaving him abandoned, and the anguished couple rushed to escape from that brazier, to go to the ranch.

The fight had stopped. The peons, before being engulfed in the flames that arose everywhere, had retreated to the ranch, the survivors of Alvin's party escaped with horse's claw, away from the tremendous danger, while the owners of the sinister place, fled in turn terrified, abandoning almost everything, since the fire's impetus was such that it had barely allowed them to extract something of the most useful and essential from their cabins.

The danger was greatly increased when the fire, spreading, reached the scattered charges of dynamite prepared for exploration.

Continuously, violent explosions were captured that made the picture more tragic, the earth jumped in volcanoes of dust and everything contributed to make the panorama more sinister.

When the small group descended towards the ranch, their eyes filled with tears and pain, when observing how the oil streams, when they caught fire, had put the fire parallel to one of the sides of the hacienda.

And this had provoked the last act of the tremendous drama. The cattle, being surprised by the fire, had gone mad and blindly threw themselves on the hawthorn tree, they had cut it off in various places, escaping in all directions to make the picture even more impressive. Virginia, who had almost fainted from shock when she watched from the ranch how the fire had broken out, seeing it run down the slopes in the direction of the ranch, had hastened to mount her jackfruit, escaping from the imminent danger she was in.

And fearing for his father's life, he had launched himself in the direction of the place of the fight, not caring what might happen to him in that blind attempt to find the rancher, to force him to retreat from the catastrophe.

And the encounter was tragically painful, when he faced Gleen, with a wounded arm and bloodstained clothes and a corpse he could not recognize, hanging limp from the chair.

Seeing Gleen and the foreman, he advanced, crying out:

"Gleen! Gleen! Out of compassion! Where is my father?

Gleen and the foreman stopped in shock, not daring to answer, but she, fixing her terrified eyes on the swaying corpse, gave an impressive cry and ran to him, hugging him with infinite despair.

-- Dad! Dad!

Gleen, ignoring her injury, came to her trying to separate her from the shattered body, while saying hoarsely:

"No one could help it, Virginia. When we were fighting with Alvin's men, your father inadvertently broke away, and with some resinous branches that he carried on his saddle, he set them on fire and threw them into the oil well. He could not avoid the expansive wave of the air when the explosion occurred and was thrown like a bullet. He killed himself crazy and nobody could help it, but if it is any consolation, I will tell you that I have killed Alvin, the monster who brought us this terrible catastrophe. At the very least, he will not profit from oil, nor will he enjoy death

"This doesn't give me back my father, Gleen, it won't even save my estate. Look, can't you see?

"I see it and I also see that the fire runs along and not across the pastures, why?

The foreman deafly stated:

"Let's go there. Here we do not solve anything and, instead, if something can be done we must try it with the men who have returned unharmed. I had something to tell you, but when we get to the ranch.

Gleen helped Virginia onto the horse and they returned to the ranch, where a dozen or more peons had returned unscathed, taking with them four more wounded in the fighting.

The foreman asked:

"What's going on? How has the fire not flowed in?

"It has been stopped by the bed of the stream that runs along the fence and the two ponds. Also, the air blows in the opposite direction.

"So, boys, you have to help the stream so that the fire cannot pass to the other side. An effort as far as our forces can go and build a barrier of earth on this side of the river, in anticipation. Take care that it does not contain dry branches or grass conducive to burning. What about livestock?

"Almost everything escaped, foreman. There are cattle at the end of the pasture, but terribly frightened. Who knows if the others have fled to the river, to sink into it, or have perished burned.

"Well, the irremediable has no remedy. We do not know what will happen, or what the end will be, but what can be saved must be saved. The only thing that seems certain is that this will never be a ranch and pasture again. The oil will kill the grass in one way or another, and the cattle, who knows what can be harvested. But everything is not lost yet, although the boss has died and his daughter is left alone in the world, her mother is in Texas, as you know, taking care of one of her sisters who is ill, and although she will not be able to avoid the terrible surprise of knowing her husband's death, at least the horror of looking at this painting will have been avoided.

Gleen and Virginia had moved Fuchs's body inside the ranch. This, at the moment, did not seem threatened of being devoured by the flames, since luck had cut off the dripping of the oil, due to the bed of the stream and the ponds.

Having made such arrangements, the foreman joined the beleaguered couple and stated:

"Mr. Gleen, you must not despise your wound. You've lost a lot of blood and you have to take care of that arm.

He shrugged his shoulders in dismay, but Virginia, reacting, exclaimed:

"Sorry, Gleen, I have been carried away by the terrible pain that my father's death has caused me and I have forgotten everything. I will heal you however I can until it is possible for a doctor to see you.

He looked for a box with medical supplies and prepared to treat the wounded man. As he did so, he looked at the foreman in anguish and muttered between hiccups:

" It's over! For us, for you and for your men.

The foreman, undecided, replied:

"That's right, we have to admit it, but I have something to communicate to you. I couldn't do it last night because of how it all came about, but now I'll tell you. Late in the afternoon, the two laborers who were working on the well that we agreed to open came very excited to tell me that they did not dare to continue digging, because the ground had become damp and the earth smelled of oil. They've gone about six yards, and it looks like the oil is about to burst. I wanted to find you to ask what we were doing, but I couldn't talk to you and I had to leave it for later. Now I let you know.

"Have you seen it? Gleen asked as they healed him.

"Yes, and I have verified that it is true. I have the conviction that, with little more that is deepened, oil will emerge, but I have understood that it should not be continued. Furthermore, I ordered to pour dirt over the hole, to keep it hidden for the time being. I didn't know how the boss was going to react and I thought that, for the moment, it was enough to know that just as there is oil in other parts of the valley, there is also here. And I understand that this is evil, the least. If the ranch is lost because cattle will no longer be able to be raised here, at least its value, or much more, you have in oil. I know they hate him like all of us, but they can always sell the land that is the largest, with what it contains of that disgusting liquid and then ... Well, not anymore, because the boss died, Miss Virginia and her mother will not be interested in continuing to raise cattle, even if it is in another place, but, at least, they will receive a good amount of money and they will not be in misery. As for us ... we'll go back to Texas and God will tell.

Virginia turned to him, saying:

"We will talk about that. My father loved you very much, you supported him, you have exposed yourself, you have risked your life to help him and defend his property and some have lost it. If you save enough to try something new, neither of you will be abandoned by me, nor by my mother. At the moment, I can not say anything. We have to wait and see how this tragedy ends, but later the future will have its last word.

"Thank you, Miss Virginia" replied the foreman, moved. You know that we all love you and that if you need us, you will have us by your side as one man. Now, I'm going to see what the boys do to ensure that the fire will not be able to reach any further and ... that fate has its last word.

Virginia finished treating her cousin's arm and, a little calmer, said:

"Gleen, I have not thanked you as I should have done for what you have done, even though you could not do more. Thanks with all my heart.

"It's not worth it, and I was forced to do that and much more. Now, all that remains for me is to arrange everything for your father's funeral, and later, if you think I can intervene in the matter of the sale of the land by negotiating with an oil company, I will do so with all my heart. I will try to confront two or more companies to dispute the land, in order to get a higher price for it and after everything is settled, you will decide what to do.

"We will study it in due course, but I also have something to ask you: what will you do?

Gleen was tense; actually, I didn't know.

"Well, I think I will have to look for a placement that allows me to finish my studies. If I was not about to finish them, I would give them up to start a new life.

"Why? If things work out financially, it is not a reason that my father has disappeared, so that we leave you hanging when what is missing is the least.

"Thank you, we cannot talk about that yet, although I am sure that what you have lost on the one hand, you will gain on the other. The important thing is what you will do afterwards. You are alone and I have the obligation to reciprocate the favors received, helping you as much as I can.

"I'm afraid you can't, Gleen.

"Why?

"Because if we sell this right away and we can't continue here, we'll go to Texas, and with the money, we'll buy another ranch. My father only wanted to defend his pastures and his cattle, I must continue his work, if it is not here in another place. Besides, I cannot leave our men abandoned, when they have exposed so much for us. I'll take them away, we'll buy a ranch, and we'll see how he defends himself. I trust at least James, who is knowledgeable and loyal.

"It is, but why the obsession? Why don't you study the proposition I made to you? By the time you are out of mourning, I may have finished my career and got a good position in some company. Now this ranch that you will have to renounce does not bind you.

"To change it for another, I have already told you. Everything will follow as closely as my father wished it, and I will follow his inspiration and, furthermore, I will not change my way of understanding life, and marriage. Whoever loves me, whoever wants to marry me, will have to follow this family tradition, as long as possible. This is an irrevocable decision, Gleen, I already told you, and it can't make a difference that my father has disappeared or that we have to go somewhere else.

Gleen, tense, muttered:

"But, Virginia, don't you realize that with my career, I can offer you something of mine and otherwise I have nowhere to drop dead? Misfortune made me live at the expense of my relatives, and if I am about to use them in life, it has been thanks to your father. Can I quit my career to offer you what? Is it not enough that I have enjoyed what is not mine? Don't you realize that loving you with all my heart, doom ties me hand and foot? The least would be to leave my studies and dedicate myself to something else, and you demand the same; What is more, is that I am a poor student.

Virginia, tense, replied:

"I don't buy husbands, Gleen. My heart has only one straight path, and to reach it, it only takes love and not money.

Gleen stiffened, staring at the fantastic landscape from there. The immense fountain of fire, continued bouncing like something infernal, marking the landscape with its parable of fire, the fires through the land, diminished as grass and spikes were consumed and nervous beings like ghosts, moved in the distance, around the burned places, looking for their properties.

Everything had been transformed, and although for the moment the losses were considerable, oil would perform the miracle of resurgence.

Gleen turned to Virginia, and, hoarsely, asked:

"Virginia ..., if I ..., I renounced everything ..., yes ..., I folded to your desire and will ... if I put myself in body and soul at your disposal to help you follow the path that you you have drawn .., wouldn't you think that I do it out of selfishness and not out of affection towards you?

 She simply replied:

"If I thought so, I would have rejected you from the first try, but you see, I don't.

They both clasped hands with emotion, while their eyes filled with tears of happiness.

END

9 798201 024420